...Regards from Camp!

#1 Getting Acquainted

... Regards from Camp!

#1
GETTING ACQUAINTED

by
Shifra Kahan Weinberg

CIS
P·U·B·L·I·S·H·E·R·S
New York · London · Jerusalem

Published and distributed
in the U.S., Canada and overseas by
C.I.S. Publishers and Distributors
180 Park Avenue, Lakewood, New Jersey 08701
(908) 905-3000 Fax: (908) 367-6666

Distributed in Israel by
C.I.S. International (Israel)
Rechov Mishkalov 18
Har Nof, Jerusalem
Tel: 02-518-935

Distributed in the U.K. and Europe by
C.I.S. International (U.K.)
89 Craven Park Road
London N15 6AH, England
Tel: 81-809-3723

Book and cover design: Deenee Cohen
Typography: Devorah Rozsansky
Cover illustration: Maureen Scullin

ISBN 1-56062-200-8 hard cover

PRINTED IN THE UNITED STATES OF AMERICA

Dedicated to my husband Moish עמ״ש and
to my children Boruch, Tehilla, Tikva, Yanki,
Shalom and Pesi עמ״ש.

Special thanks to my daughter Tehilla, gymnastics counselor extraordinaire, who was my
first proofreader and whose input was essential
in the creation of this series.

A great big *yasher koach* to Raizy Kaufman,
Deenee Cohen and the entire fantastic staff at
C.I.S. Publishers for their professionalism and
encouragement in nuturing this series from the
germ of an idea to fruition.

Table of Contents

Chapter 1   En Route 11

Chapter 2   Settling In 25

Chapter 3   Fright in the Night............................ 41

Chapter 4   Bunk Inspection Blues 54

Chapter 5   Kitchen Capers 69

Chapter 6   Soapsuds in the Morning 81

Chapter 7   Forward March 97

Chapter 8   Cascading Currents 116

Chapter 9   Victory in Sight 130

Chapter 10 Ten Happy Campers...................... 148

             Glossary 167

CHAPTER ONE

En Route

Tzippi pivoted in her seat to get a good view of the rowdy group of girls on the chartered Trailways bus. "This is the life!" she murmured happily to herself.

She pulled a tattered, dog-eared calendar out of her travelling bag and hugged it to her chest. A whole year of longing was contained in its wrinkled pages.

Tzippi leafed through the months reluctantly spent in school. Each sheet bore scrawled rows of big black X's. She had been counting down all winter for this moment to arrive. Now that it was here, she could hardly wait for the rest of the day to get underway.

The girls were draped over the backs of the seats, sprawled in the aisles, even hanging from the roof, if you counted those who were swinging to and fro using the loops hanging from the overhead racks. A sense of celebration was in the air. Conversations were being carried out above and beyond any decibel level known to the human race. Snippets of songs were circulating through the general pandemonium.

"Ah, camp," Tzippi purred contentedly, stroking her faithful calendar, on which the date June 28 was circled in pink and yellow fluorescent markers.

Suddenly, Tzippi heard a familiar voice raised in song.

"Camp Tehila you're the best,
Head and shoulders above the rest,
Summer's here and we're set for a treat,
For *ruach* and fun that can't be beat."

That voice could belong to only one person! Sure enough, there on the seat directly in front of her was Yehudis, hands clapping and feet stomping as she belted out one of the theme songs from last year. Tzippi smiled to herself. It was so much fun being an old-timer at camp!

"Hi, Yehudis!" Tzippi leaned over the front of her seat and punched Yehudis good-naturedly on the arm. "Sounds like you've still got the loudest voice in camp!"

"Yup," Yehudis giggled proudly, "the loudest and the greatest!"

Tzippi tried as hard as she could to suppress her smile. Yehudis sure had the loudest voice in camp, but the reason it was so easily identifiable as pure Yehudis and no one else was because it was so off-key; no one else in the world, Tzippi was convinced, could murder the tune of a song quite the way Yehudis could.

"Hey, Tzippi!" Yehudis called cheerfully. "You got anything new up your sleeve for this year?"

"Are you kidding? I've been planning for months! Wait till

you see what I've dreamed up for this season!"

Tzippi chortled as she replayed in her mind some of her exploits from previous summers. It was not for nothing that counselors in-the-know whispered to all newcomers on staff, "When you're around Tzipporah Laya Zandberg, *watch out!*"

The only reason Tzippi had been able to evade serious retribution for her shenanigans was that she timed her best pranks for just before important intercamp sports meets. Camp Tehila was a very competitive place, and Tzippi was fabulous at almost every sport played in camp. The head counselors needed her on their team, and that was why she had never been sent home from camp in disgrace, although the possibility had been under consideration several times over the years.

As the scenery of New York's suburbs flashed by the bus windows, Tzippi settled comfortably into her seat. Not for her the wild strap hanging or seat hopping! She had to gather her reserve energy for when it would be needed most.

Fondly fingering her tattered calendar, Tzippi daydreamed placidly, conserving her strength. She had to be in top form when the bus pulled into the driveway of camp and disgorged its passengers. And she had only about an hour and a half of tranquility left before she was ready to launch herself full force into another frantic summer at Camp Tehila.

Libby toyed nervously with the buckle of her seatbelt. The plane had not even lifted off the ground, and the stewardess was already describing all the perils the passengers might encounter on this trip. From rough weather to forced landings in the ocean, the possibilities were too horrible to contemplate. Libby watched numbly as the flight attendant demonstrated the proper usage of depressurization face masks and pointed out the locations of the life rafts and life jackets.

"How am I ever going to remember all this stuff?" Libby fretted as she concentrated on committing to memory the correct way to inflate each lifesaving device.

Swivelling her head to the right, Libby observed her seatmate leaning forward and reaching into the pocket attached to the back of the seat in front of him. He extracted a plastic-coated card, adjusted the glasses on the bridge of his nose and proceeded to examine the words and diagrams with scrupulous care.

Looks like something important, Libby speculated. I'd better see what that is.

Libby extended her arm and reached into the pouch before her. She found the card and pulled it out, scrutinizing the brightly colored brochure with interest. Her interest turned to alarm when she realized that the card just featured more details and full color illustrations of the hazards being dramatized by the stewardess in the aisle. It also pointed out the emergency exits, and Libby was somewhat relieved to see that at least she was seated reasonably close to a red EXIT sign.

Rummaging around some more in the pouch, Libby turned up a magazine and a strange paper bag with a waxy inside and drawstrings on the top. It said: TO BE USED IN CASE OF AIR-SICKNESS. Libby hadn't realized until that very moment that her stomach was feeling sort of queasy.

The plane gave a shudder as its engine burst into life. Clutching the handrests of her seat, Libby could feel the plane pick up speed rapidly as it hurtled down the runway. She chewed conscientiously on the wad of gum in her mouth, which had by now pretty much lost its flavor. Her parents had instructed her to keep chewing the gum all during the takeoff so that her ears wouldn't pop, and she was taking this advice very seriously. Visions of people's ears exploding into smithereens around her waltzed whimsically through her brain as the plane left the ground and angled upward.

I am not going to be airsick, I am not going to be airsick, Libby repeated relentlessly to herself. She fervently hoped that she wouldn't disgrace herself by actually having to make use of that awful bag. Just in case, though, she made sure it was tucked at the side of her seat, so that it would be instantly available should the unthinkable happen.

As soon as the plane seemed to be levelling off, and Libby discovered with relief that she so far had two intact, though kind of stuffed up, ears and an empty airsickness bag, she leaned back into the tapestried upholstery of her seat and watched the flight attendants making their way down the aisle with drinks.

Out the window, the sun was streaming brilliantly onto a fantasy world of snow-white, fluffy clouds floating over an aquamarine stretch of ocean. Miami was getting further and further away as the Boeing 747 headed north toward New York.

Libby twisted a lock of bright golden hair around her finger as she fantasized about what her first experience in overnight camp would be like. She had never been out of the state of Florida, and now she was headed for the Catskill Mountains, to the place where her mother had spent many happy summers as a girl, a destination called Camp Tehila.

In Libby's mind's eye, a dainty scene came to mind, drawn from her experience with Miami architecture: a neat circle of stucco bungalows, their smooth surfaces washed in pretty pastel shades of pink and green, surrounding a big open field. She visualized the corrugated red roofs of each bungalow glinting in the bright sunlight of a New York summer and tidy shutters framing each window.

Libby sighed in contentment after the initial fright of her solo flight had passed, and she was the proud possessor of a still empty airsickness bag.

"I can't wait to get to camp!" she said aloud.

The van, crammed with luggage, was on the New York State Thruway, when Shalva came to a disturbing realization.

"I don't *want* to go to camp."

Admittedly, it was a little late in the planning process to have come to this conclusion. The van had been on the road for nearly four hours since its departure from Toronto, not counting the one-hour stop in Niagara Falls for a quick shopping trip and a snack.

How did I ever let them talk me into it? she puzzled, turning the thought over and over in her mind.

Three weeks before, Shalva had been engrossed in studying for finals. She'd been thrilled that for once she had no structured plans whatsoever for the summer. After years of being imprisoned in day camps, she was looking forward to just taking each day as it came. Visions of lazy days sprawled on a lawn chair in the backyard with a good book and a pitcher of ice-cold lemonade danced in her head. Next year she would probably apply as a junior counselor in the day camp; this would be the only vacation in which she would retain the absolute freedom to do whatever she wanted from morning to night.

And then her parents had come home from the office and dropped their bombshell at the precise moment when she was least prepared to deal with it—the night before her final math exam. She replayed the scene in her memory:

Mom (doling out portions of Caesar Salad): "By the way, Shalva, there's a conference coming up the first week of July in San Francisco."

Shalva: "Mm. Are there any more croutons left?"

Mom (passing the container of croutons): "Dad and I thought it would be beneficial for us professionally if we were there."

Shalva (her nose buried in the math book spread in front of her on the table; books weren't usually allowed at the dinner table, but during finals her parents relented): "Mm. Good salad, Mom."

Dad: "And since we'd already be a good part of the way there, we figure we can kill two birds with one stone by hopping over to the Far East to see the supplier that we were planning on checking out in early September. That way, we won't have to worry about the trip getting too close to the *Yamim Tovim*."

Shalva (her brow furrowed in concentration as she tries to determine the solution to a particularly difficult problem): "That's nice. Can you pass the garlic bread?"

Mom: "So we signed you up for four weeks at a really lovely camp in the mountains."

Shalva (chewing garlic bread, as the light dawns and her solution to the knotty problem finally matches the one in the answer guide): "That's *great*! I can't believe I finally got the right answer to this!"

And so her parents had, true to their words, made their

airline reservations to coincide with the day camp would begin. They ordered printed name tapes and an extra large hockey bag. Arrangements were made for the grass to be trimmed and the newspaper delivery stopped. Shalva's mother was on the phone making reservations for a rental van when Shalva came home from school in a jubilant mood the next day.

"Are we going somewhere during vacation?" Shalva asked her mother curiously. "I thought you said we were going to hang around the house."

Mrs. Silverstein's eyes widened in surprise. "Of course we're going somewhere," she reminded Shalva in a puzzled voice. "We discussed it all at the dinner table last night. Dad and I are going to California and the Far East, and you're going to camp."

"Camp?" Shalva shrieked in alarm. "Which camp?"

"The really nice camp in the Catskill Mountains I told you about last night," Mrs. Silverstein replied, getting more perplexed by the minute. "It's called Camp Tehila."

"An overnight camp?" Shalva screeched. "We discussed that I would be going to an overnight camp?"

"Certainly," Mrs. Silverstein nodded forcefully. "We knew you were planning on spending the summer vegetating in the backyard. That's why we *asked* you if camp would be okay. You said very clearly that camp would be fine. In fact, I distinctly recall that you thought the idea was 'great'!"

"Oh, brother!" Shalva groaned, her heart sinking.

But what could she do? The plans were signed, sealed and just about engraved in stone. Shalva decided to ignore the whole idea, and maybe, by some stroke of luck, her parents would change their plans at the last minute.

About a week before D-Day (departure day, that is), the stark reality of her predicament hit Shalva like a sharp blow to the kidneys. It was triggered by a question posed to her at breakfast.

"Shalva, when are you planning on packing your bags?" her mother wondered. "Everything's all labelled. There are only five more days until we have to leave."

Resignedly, Shalva set about throwing her belongings together into a pile in the middle of her room. With the camp list in her hand, she poked and prodded at the mess, selecting the necessities for her upcoming four-week exile.

She had reassured herself uneasily that she could certainly manage to cope with four measly weeks at sleepaway camp. After all, there would still be another whole month of vacation left when she got back. But now that she was actually on her way, the miles flowing swiftly by as the van got further and further from Toronto, Shalva was having second thoughts.

"I just know that I'm going to *hate* camp!" Shalva griped vehemently, tossing her auburn ponytail back over her shoulder. "Especially a camp where I don't know a living soul! How am I ever going to survive the next four weeks?"

"Hurry up. We're going to be late!"

Margalit leaned into the ornate doorway of her family's stately mansion in Lawrence, Long Island and peered anxiously up the lushly carpeted steps of the entrance hallway.

"Don't worry, missy, we're coming," Maria called cheerfully from somewhere upstairs. A huge suitcase lumbered into view on the second floor landing.

"How many more are there anyway?" Margalit demanded

fretfully. "The whole trunk's full!"

"Just two more left now. We're almost done. Why don't you just go into the breakfast room and have another glass of freshly-squeezed orange juice till we're ready?"

"I already had two glasses of juice." Margalit stamped her foot. "Look what time it is!"

With an impatient scowl obscuring her pretty features, Margalit watched the huge piece of luggage make its way down the stairs and out the door. Unbidden, a tiny smile played at the corners of her lips. Dominic, the gardener, had come in to give Maria a hand. Clad in his coveralls, a weeding fork hanging out of his back pocket, he handled the suitcases as if they were giant potted palms, gripping them from below as he staggered along. This position made the suitcases appear to be walking by themselves, perched on the gardener's long, lanky legs. It was truly a sight to behold, and if she hadn't been so disturbed at being late again, she probably would have burst into uproarious gales of laughter.

Margalit glanced anxiously at the gleaming Rolex watch on her wrist. She had wanted desperately to take the regular camp bus with the rest of the girls, but as it so often happened lately, her parents were out of town on business. Maria was burdened with so much extra work during their absence that she had not had the suitcases ready when the luggage van had stopped by to pick them up. Since Albert was going to drive the luggage up to camp anyway in the big limousine, Maria had gaily packed a picnic lunch and urged Margalit to go along for the ride and make a fun day of it.

Never having been to overnight camp before, Margalit had no way of knowing that six overstuffed designer suitcases and duffles were a bit more than the average camper would be bringing to camp. Maria had taken the camp list and generously quadrupled the number of each item specified. She had also embellished the list with touches of her own, so that Margalit would not be deprived of any of the creature comforts of home.

As the silver limousine pulled away from the circular driveway fronting the Rothman residence, Margalit glanced through its tinted window and caught sight of Maria, clad in a duster and pink fluffy slippers, waving vigorously from behind the foliage on the porch.

"Are you comfortable back there, Miss Margalit?" Albert inquired in his stilted British accent.

Margalit was sharing the back of the limousine with an overnight case and a large duffle bag which had not fit into the ordinarily spacious trunk. Still, the plush back seat had so much legroom that there was plenty of space for Margalit to stretch out without either piece cramping her in the slightest.

"Thanks, Albert, I'm fine," Margalit responded politely.

Now that they were finally on their way, Margalit sank into the soft gray velour and wondered what camp would be like. She'd never been away from home alone before, although she'd travelled all over the world on numerous occasions with her family. The kids at school had been making such a fuss about their upcoming adventures at camp that Margalit had yearned to go too. Her parents had been skeptical. But Margalit had persisted, and eventually, they had given in.

I wonder if Camp Tehila will be anything like the day camp in that fancy hotel in Switzerland I stayed at while Mommy and Totti attended their business meetings. Margalit ran her fingers through her long, shiny black hair and dreamily remembered the deliciously prepared meals, the multitude of activities, the crystal clear lake.

She was slowly drifting off to sleep (she'd been so excited about her first stay at camp that she'd barely slept a wink all night) when her reverie was interrupted by the buzzing of the cellular phone. There was a short pause, and then Albert called to her from the driver's seat.

"Telephone call for you, Miss Margalit."

"For *me*?" Margalit's big blue eyes widened in wonder as she reached for the phone. She removed the receiver from its cradle and held it tentatively to her ear.

"Hello, hello," someone was saying. "Margalit, are you there?"

"Hi," Margalit squeaked nervously. She couldn't remember if she had ever gotten a call on the gleaming plum-colored car phone before.

"Margalit, can you hear me?"

Margalit strained to identify the voice on the other end of the line. There was a lot of static.

The voice hesitated and then another voice came on. "Margie, darling, can't you hear us well?"

A flood of relief washed over Margalit. "Mommy, is that you?"

"Yes, darling. Totti and I wanted to wish you luck on your first day all by yourself in Camp Tehila."

"Thanks, Ma."

"And we wanted to repeat what we told you before we left. If you have any problems at all, be sure to call home and Albert will come right out and get you."

"I'm sure I won't have any problems!" Margalit announced

confidently. Then, with a smile, she added, "I'm a big girl now, remember?"

"And if Maria forgot to pack you anything, just call home, and someone will arrange to get it to you."

This caused Margalit to erupt in a fit of hysterical laughter.

"Did I say something funny?" Mrs. Rothman was puzzled.

Margalit giggled uncontrollably. Then, remembering it was a long distance call, she took a deep breath and explained, "Mom, Maria packed so much stuff, there's probably nothing left in the house any more! I can't believe she could have forgotten anything!"

"But if she did . . ."

"Right. If she did, I'll call. Don't worry so much!"

"Margalit?" Mr. Rothman was talking now. Margalit strained to hear, as the static had started again, and his voice was fading in and out.

"Yes?"

"There's a surprise in your suitcase," Mr. Rothman revealed, sounding proud.

Suitcase? Margalit wondered if her parents knew that right now she was on her way to camp with a perfectly matched set of *six* designer pieces.

"What is it?" she wondered, her excitement mounting.

"It's your very own cellular phone! Anytime you get lonesome and want to talk to Mommy or me, you can call home. If we're not there, Maria will know where we are; she can get in touch with us, and we'll call you."

"Wow! That's great! Thanks a million!"

"Bye now, Margie."

"Bye."

Margalit replaced the telephone in its cradle and stared at the newly planted fields flashing past the limousine's windows.

"I *am* going to have a wonderful time at camp," she reassured herself firmly. "Everybody else at school does. Why shouldn't I?"

CHAPTER TWO

Settling In

By the time the first Trailways bus pulled into the driveway of Camp Tehila, loaded with its boisterously singing occupants, Libby had already been in camp almost twelve hours.

When her parents had seen her off at the airport, they had given her the Bunk Assignment Card she had received in the mail, and assured her that someone from camp would meet her when she disembarked from the plane. All through the flight, Libby had worried about what would happen if she got off the plane and nobody was there. Luckily, her fears had proved groundless.

Heading out into the departure lounge, the first person Libby noticed was a teenager dressed in a long denim skirt and a three-quarter sleeved top. Among the tank tops and shorts, her outfit stood out to Libby like a welcome beacon. The modestly dressed teenager turned out to be a counselor, who had also just arrived in New York, but from Los Angeles. The two of them walked down dozens of seemingly endless corridors until they reached the luggage pickup area. There, they joined over a dozen girls from various parts of the United States and Canada, in addition to a waitress from Belgium and a lifeguard from England.

The girls were all tired after their journeys. They had been sitting on their suitcases, waiting for Libby's flight to arrive. Now that she was here, they perked up and took turns showing her how to snatch her bags off the conveyor belt of the luggage carousel. Standing beside her retrieved baggage, Libby watched in alarm as the parcels not immediately grabbed by their owners completed the circuit of the luggage pickup area and were swallowed up by a yawning hole in the wall.

Wondering what had happened to the unlucky items that disappeared into the mysterious void, Libby gripped her own suitcase and duffle bag and hauled them over to the pile of others soon to be headed to Camp Tehila.

The counselor from California, whose name was Chassida, excused herself to make a call. Not long after, a little yellow school bus pulled up at the curb. The driver, a short woman wearing a frizzy red *sheitel*, honked her horn repeatedly. When she saw that this was not eliciting any response from the cluster of chatting girls inside the terminal, she leaned out of the doorway of the bus and flapped her arms frantically, trying desperately to attract their attention.

"Look at that ridiculous lady," a loud voice bellowed from somewhere in the arrivals lounge. "She thinks she's a chicken!"

Heads turned, and other travellers joined the first in mocking laughter. The Camp Tehila campers-to-be interrupted their conversation and curiously peered through the large plate glass window to observe the object of scorn. Chassida leaped up in concern as she realized who it was.

"It's Bessie the camp driver. Hurry! Grab your stuff and dash out to the bus!" Chassida was flustered that she hadn't noticed the bus pull up.

"What's she doing?"

"She does look kind of like a funny fowl."

"Hey, this stuff is heavy. Why the rush?"

As the jumbled mass of girls and bags tumbled onto the bus, they could see the cause of the little woman's consternation. A hulking policeman, sporting a massive scowl and waving a ticket pad, was bustling straight in their direction. Bessie slammed the door of the bus shut and stepped on the gas just as the officer pulled alongside.

"Hey lady! No stopping!" the fellow blustered furiously. "Whaddaya think this is, a bus stop or something?"

"Whew, that was close!" Chassida exclaimed.

"*Baruch Hashem*!" Bessie agreed. She produced a large handkerchief from her pocket and mopped her profusely sweating face.

As the bus turned onto the highway, bound for the Catskill Mountains, the exhausted girls thankfully leaned their heads on their seats and closed their eyes. Within minutes, though, they were startled to hear strains of music coming from the front of the bus.

"Sounds like a guitar!" Libby observed to her seatmate.

The girl tilted her head to the side and listened very attentively.

"Yup. That's Chassida," she replied, beginning to snap her

fingers to the beat. "She was the head of band last summer, and boy, can she strum a tune!"

Clapping and singing now joined the twanging of the guitar, and before long, the *ruach* had affected the back of the bus as well. The trip to camp was filled with song and laughter as the counselors tried to imbue the travellers with Camp Tehila spirit.

The little yellow bus pulled into the driveway of camp just in time for supper. The girls were escorted into the dining room, where they were cheerfully greeted by Hindy, the head counselor, and served a hot meal. Their luggage, some of which had already travelled almost halfway around the world, was unceremoniously shoved beside the tower of assorted suitcases and duffle bags heaped on the lawn in front of the main house.

After a fine meal of hamburgers and baked potatoes, the sated travellers spilled out of the dining hall to reclaim their belongings and find their bunkhouses. Huffing and puffing, they latched onto their possessions one last time.

Libby turned out to be the first occupant of Bunk Achva, and she got first pick of bunks and cubbies. It was pretty lonesome in the bunkhouse that night, although two waitresses came to share it with her. First thing in the morning, though, Libby took herself for a mini-tour of Camp Tehila.

As she strolled leisurely around the almost deserted campgrounds, Libby saw enough to convince herself that she had made the right decision. From handball court to swimming pool, Camp Tehila looked like it was going to be a really fun place to spend the summer!

"Last one off is a moldy marshmallow!" Tzippi announced to one and all as she elbowed her way to the front of the bus.

The door of the bus slowly swung open, discharging a stream of happy, babbling girls. Hindy, the head counselor, stood at the edge of the driveway calling out directions. She chanced to look toward the entrance of the bus just as Tzippi was hurtling through. Camper's and counselor's eyes met.

"Well, well, if it isn't Tzipporah Laya Zandberg!" Hindy observed, her enthusiasm slightly dimmed.

"Hiya Hindy!" Tzippi replied exuberantly. "You the head counselor this year?"

"Yes I am. You wouldn't by any chance have grown up since last year, Tzipporah Laya?"

Tzippi grinned from ear to ear. "Not a chance!" She chuckled merrily.

Hindy rolled her eyes as Tzippi made her way through the crowd of girls. Everyone seemed to know her, and she had something to say to each girl.

A chubby girl with thick glasses elbowed Tzippi as she was cruising past. "Hey, Tzip," she called, eyeing Tzippi's new wedge cut. "It looks like you got a haircut since last year."

"Uh huh! How do you like the new me?" Tzippi whirled around so the girls could admire her hairdo from all angles.

"Hope it's as much fun as the old you!" Yehudis grinned as she went by.

"So why'd you cut it anyway?" a tall, thin blonde inquired curiously. Tzippi's long, flaming red curls had been her trademark for years.

"Aw, you know," Tzippi shrugged. "I got tired of looking like Bozo the Clown!"

Tzippi cheerfully made her way through the teeming crowds to the tower of luggage on the lawn.

"Last one to find her stuff is a . . ." Tzippi stood on tiptoes and issued her challenge to the others, trying to think of a new pair of words she had not used before. "Last one to find her stuff is a . . . barbecued banana!"

Tzippi, of course, was not the last one to find her suitcases. That was because she went through this procedure enough times and added a little something to her chances for success. Both of her duffles were adorned with huge silver stars made of puffy fabric paint. They stood out from the crowd like spaceships in the middle of a crowded highway during rush hour.

As Tzippi was hauling her distinctive belongings out of the mess on the lawn, and the rest of the girls were doggedly pawing through the pile searching for their own stuff, a stretch limousine was pulling up in the camp driveway.

"Tzippi, get a load of that!" Chumi squealed. Her eyes were as round as saucers as she tugged on Tzippi's arm to draw her attention to the newest arrival.

"Wow!" Tzippi gasped. "Hey, everyone, look at that!"

All eyes turned to the girl with long, swinging black hair emerging from the back seat of the elegant car. The furious activity of luggage sorting suddenly ceased and the recently arrived New Yorkers stared in awe, mouths agape, at the magnificent silver vehicle.

"It's like Cinderella at the ball," Malky whispered.

Uncomfortable at all of the attention she was drawing, Margalit said the first thing that came to mind. "Whatsamatter? You guys never saw a limo before?"

She was sorry almost as soon as the last word left her mouth. Embarrassed, she ducked back into the limousine and started to yank at her duffle bag.

"Oh no. Let me do that for you, Miss Margalit," Albert offered gallantly.

"Miss Margalit?" Malky echoed. She couldn't believe her ears! It really *was* like Cinderella at the ball!

"Listen, Albert," Margalit whispered, wrestling the heavy Gucci duffle out of the limousine. "I can take care of this duffle myself."

"Oh no, Miss Margalit. That would be unpardonable of me. Here, let me have it!"

The New Yorkers watched the scene unfold in disbelief. An unnatural calm descended on Camp Tehila as all ears strained to catch traces of this fascinating dialogue.

Hindy had been busy clearing a space in the parking lot for the Baltimore bus, which was due to arrive any moment. She realized that something was amiss when the general pandemonium that had been rampant in the camp suddenly tapered off. Hurrying up the driveway, she came upon the newly arrived camper and her chauffeur wrestling with a piece of luggage beside a magnificent, silver stretch limousine.

"What seems to be the trouble?" Hindy asked sweetly.

"Nothing!" Margalit could feel a hideous red flush creeping across her cheeks. The one thing she had absolutely *not* wanted to do was make a spectacle of herself. How she wished she could have been on the regular camp bus with all the other girls!

Hindy draped an arm around Margalit's shoulders. "Let's see your Bunk Assignment Card," she invited in what she hoped was a suitably head-counselory tone.

Margalit appeared confused, but Albert came to the rescue with a crisp white envelope, which he handed to Hindy in his gloved hand. Hindy scrutinized the card inside.

"Okay, Margalit," she smiled warmly, "you're in Bunk Achva. That's right up the hill and over to the left. Why don't you leave your things in this pile on the lawn? One of the maintenance men will be along shortly to help you up with the stuff you can't manage yourself."

Holding back her tears, which were threatening to spill out in a torrent, Margalit said in a very low voice, "I *can't* put these bags on the dirty grass. My mother would have a fit! They're from her Gucci collection!"

"Oh, I see," Hindy said brightly, although she really didn't see at all. "Okay, then why don't you just carry those two pieces up to the bunkhouse yourself? Can you manage?"

"Sure," Margalit agreed enthusiastically. She didn't dare mention that the two pieces Hindy had seen in the back seat of the car were the smallest and lightest of the lot.

"That's settled then." Hindy heaved a sigh of relief. "See you later."

"Did you hear that?" Malky declared reverently. "She's in Bunk Achva."

"You're kidding!" Tzippi crowed. "So am I! Hey, you guys, who else around here's in Bunk Achva?"

Bunk Assignment Cards were produced and scanned with care. There were shouts of glee and sighs of disappointment.

Yehudis appeared at Tzippi's side and gestured to the man in the full chauffeur's uniform and the black-haired girl struggling up the hill with an endless assortment of baggage.

"So, Tzippi, old buddy," she chirped joyfully. "It's me and you and *her*."

"And I," announced a cheerful Russian girl who now joined the pair.

"Also me," said Yaffa as she joined the trio and grinned happily at Tzippi. "It looks like we're going to have a mighty interesting bunk this year, folks!"

"I'm Nava," a slender girl with her hair gathered into a bushy brown ponytail introduced herself. "My card says Bunk Achva, too. Sorry, but I don't know any of your names."

"That's easily remedied." Tzippi curtsied with a flourish and announced, "Presenting Her Royal Highness Tzipporah Laya Zandberg! Tzippi, to my friends."

"Olga," the Russian girl identified herself.

"And these are Yehudis and Yaffa, the Double Y's. We're all old hands at this camp." Tzippi stopped to catch her breath. "Who else? Step right up to the best bunk in the entire mountains!"

"I'm in Bunk Achva, too," declared a pretty girl with shoulder-length blonde hair held off her face by a fabric headband. "And I've been here since last night."

"Oh my gosh, I almost forgot," Tzippi cried. "Let's get a move on it! All the best bunks and cubbies will be gone in no time flat!" She slung her duffle bag over her shoulder, grabbed her suitcase and began huffing and puffing her way up the hill to the bunkhouse.

The clamor resumed as the search for missing belongings continued. Just as the first batch of girls were getting themselves sorted out, two more buses pulled into the parking lot and the bedlam started all over again.

"ALL COUNSELORS PLEASE REPORT TO THE DINING HALL. COUNSELORS REPORT TO THE DINING HALL IMMEDIATELY!"

The announcement reverberated in the air as several cars and vans were simultaneously pulling into the parking lot. Girls of all sizes, accompanied by a wide assortment of family members, spilled out to join the general melee.

"Whew, I'm just in time!" Chedva grabbed a huge sports bag, kissed her married sister good-bye and made a beeline for the dining hall. Puffing and panting, she arrived just as the meeting was being called to order.

Hindy kicked off the gathering with a little speech about the responsibilities and rewards of being a counselor. Chedva shoved her brightly colored bag against the wall and grabbed a chair. She had been to Camp Tehila for so many summers that she had lost count, and she'd been both a junior counselor and a regular counselor, so she knew this spiel practically by heart. The important part would come later, when the bunk assignment lists would be handed out. She waited patiently.

"And now," Hindy concluded, after the camp mother and nurse had been introduced, "here's what you've all been waiting for!"

She thumbed through a stack of papers and began walking around the room handing sheets out. When she got to Chedva, she couldn't help but remark, "I'm sure glad it's you who's been assigned to Bunk Achva. That one's going to be a real challenge!"

Chedva smiled up at Hindy. I wonder what she means by that, she thought uneasily to herself.

Dragging her bag down the steps of the dining hall on the way to the Achva bunkhouse, Chedva decided to peruse the list of Achva campers one more time. Perhaps she would find a clue to Hindy's strange comment.

". . . Margalit Rothman . . . Shalva Silverstein . . . Yaffa
Steinfeld . . . Miriam Tauber . . ." Chedva read as she tugged
at her bag. She had just about made it down the entire flight of
steps when she caught her breath and momentarily lost her
footing. Righting herself at the last minute, she stared, appalled,
at the last name on the alphabetically arranged list. Tzipporah
Laya Zandberg, red-headed mischief-maker par excellence! To
a counselor, this was the most feared name in Camp Tehila!

"Any more sandwiches, Mom?"
Shalva had been taking a nap, sprawled across an entire
bench in the van. The moment she opened her eyes, the first
thought in her mind had been of food.
"No, honey. You've already eaten three egg salad sandwiches on toast, three tuna fish sandwiches on rye, two bagels
with cream cheese and lox and a dozen chocolate croissants.
We're totally cleaned out."
"But I'm starving!" Shalva wailed. "We've been on the road
forever!"
"Well, there's nowhere to stop around here," Mr. Silverstein
explained regretfully, gesturing to a sign whizzing by at the side
of the highway. It read, "NO SERVICES ALONG THIS ROUTE."
The van had raced through Binghamton, the last major city
on their itinerary, almost an hour before. According to Mr.
Silverstein's calculations, they should be approaching the camp
fairly soon. Then it would be only about two more hours until
he and his wife reached their hotel in Manhattan, and that put
him into a very jolly mood indeed. He leaned back in his seat and
hummed a Yiddish tune as he tried to comfort his exasperated
daughter.

"Although this stretch of Route 17 is almost deserted," Mr. Silverstein boomed in a sing-song voice, as if he were reviewing a piece of *Gemara*, "we should be hitting the Catskill Mountains in . . ."

He turned inquisitively to his wife, who was peering at a large map of the state of New York. Jabbing a thick thumb in the direction of the billowing sheet, Mr. Silverstein knit his brows and wondered aloud, "*Nu?* In how long do you think?"

"It looks like about thirty miles," Mrs. Silverstein answered thoughtfully. The map rustled loudly as she ran her finger along the bright yellow line that she had highlighted before they left. "We should be hitting the turn-off to Camp Tehila within half an hour."

Shalva bit her lip. "Any veggies left?"

"Not even a pepper!"

"Potato chips? We couldn't have finished both bags!"

"Afraid so."

The situation was getting desperate. "Isn't there *anything* at all left?"

Mrs. Silverstein shifted the map in her lap and a doughnut materialized beneath it. She handed it to Shalva, who thanked her mother profusely and wolfed down the cinnamon coated delight in two bites.

"Think they'll still be serving supper when we get to the camp?"

"I don't see why not. It's only six o'clock. We should be there in an hour, tops."

"Good!" said Shalva, satisfied. She settled back into the comfortable upholstery of her seat, tapping her foot in tune to the Jewish music playing on the van's tape deck.

About thirty-five minutes later, just as her parents had predicted, the van turned off the highway at the Swan Lake exit.

"Okay, hold your hats. We're almost there!" Mr. Silverstein announced at the end of the ramp. He turned to his wife. "Where to from here?"

Mrs. Silverstein scratched her head, perplexed. "That's funny. We only have directions to the proper exit off the highway. After that, there's nothing here!"

"Well, we've gotten all the way from Toronto to the Catskill Mountains. There are probably no further directions because the camp is so easy to find."

"I hope so."

"I hope *not*," Shalva whispered under her breath. If they couldn't find the camp, she wouldn't have to go. Maybe they'd feel so sorry for her not having a place to stay that they'd take her with them to California.

As Shalva dreamed of skipping through the sand with the Pacific Ocean roaring in the background and of strolling happily through Disneyland wedged between her thrilled parents, the van hurtled down one country road after another.

"Have either of you seen any signs for Camp Tehila?" Mrs. Silverstein peered uneasily through the tinted glass of the van window. All she could see was an unbroken line of trees.

"Not yet. But it must be on this road somewhere," Mr. Silverstein replied confidently.

"It's getting dark, Dad," Shalva noted, catching sight of the flaming red sun sinking behind a bank of purple clouds.

"Oh, no! Thanks for reminding me. We'd better pull off somewhere so I can *daven Minchah.*"

"Shouldn't we at least stop at a gas station?" Mrs. Silverstein wondered aloud. She anxiously twisted the map in her lap.

"When was the last time you saw a gas station?"

Mrs. Silverstein fluttered her hands nervously and tried to remember. "Let's see now. It must have been at least twenty minutes ago," she guessed.

"There goes supper," Shalva muttered. She could feel the first twinges of hunger rumbling in her empty stomach. The tense mood in the car was contagious, and she was getting increasingly jittery.

The van pulled over to the side of the road and parked near what appeared to be a forest of trees. Under the heavy green canopy of their leaves, the dark was closing in fast. Mr. Silverstein reached for the pouch in the glove compartment which contained his *siddur* and compass. While he *davened*, Mrs. Silverstein re-examined her map.

"The small country roads are so tiny on here," she grumbled, trying to trace the thin lines with her finger. "I can hardly make them out. We could wander these roads all night and not find the camp." She was very tired from the long trip and getting more distressed by the minute.

"What happens if we can't find it?" Shalva asked quietly.

Swallowing her doubts, Mrs. Silverstein smiled reassuringly at her restless daughter. "Oh, we'll find it all right," she remarked brightly. Then she added under her breath, "I hope!"

By the time Mr. Silverstein had finished *Minchah*, night was falling fast. If it had been hard to locate things on the remote country roads in the light, it was almost impossible to see anything in the dark. There were no lights on the roadway; only orange reflector strips illuminated the sides of the lanes.

Suddenly, Shalva spotted a large building on the left side of the road. "Wait! That looks familiar!" she called excitedly from the back seat.

Her parents both turned to look at the brightly lit hotel.

"Oh my goodness, do you know why that looks familiar?" Mrs. Silverstein asked her husband in despair.

"No. Why?"

"Because we went past it about twenty-five minutes ago!"

Mr. Silverstein backed up into the nearest driveway and headed back to the hotel. "I'll run up to the office and ask for directions," he said, not quite as cheerful as he had been before.

Ten minutes later, Mr. Silverstein returned to the van and reported, "We must have passed the turnoff to Camp Tehila half a dozen times! The lady in the office knows where it is because she has a niece there. She says the road isn't marked, but that once you find it, you'll never forget it."

By this time, Shalva was bone-tired. If she had to be stuck in Camp Tehila for four weeks, she sure hoped they'd get there soon.

At almost nine o'clock, when the maroon van with Toronto plates finally pulled into the Camp Tehila driveway, Hindy was sitting on the steps of the main house, winding down after the busy first day. She stared as the van stopped and a man, a lady and a young girl spilled out.

"Uh oh," she murmured, "it looks like there's still one more!" And she scurried down to the new arrival to direct her and her parcels to the correct bunkhouse.

Shalva arrived at the Achva bunkhouse while the rest of its residents were still out at night activity. There was only one bed left and, of course, it was the least desirable one. Nonetheless, it *was* a place to lay her exhausted head. Shalva collapsed onto the lumpy mattress and bid her parents a bon voyage.

It wasn't too long before the chill in the bunkhouse began to penetrate her thin pullover. Shivering, Shalva slid off the unadorned mattress and began poking around in her mammoth hockey bag. She extricated her sleeping bag and a pillow and plopped them haphazardly on the cot. Then she located a pair of warm flannel pajamas and hastily readied herself for bed. She was just crawling in and getting comfortable as the rest of the members of Bunk Achva were chummily climbing the hill to the bunkhouse.

"What a great beginning," Shalva mumbled to herself as she wrapped the sleeping bag tightly around her shoulders. "Worst bed! Freezing night! And no supper!"

CHAPTER THREE

Fright in the Night

As night approached, the temperature started to plummet. Campers and counselors attended night activity clad in their heaviest sweaters. Despite being well bundled, by the time night activity was over and they were back in their bunkhouse, the girls of Bunk Achva were chilled to the bone.

Margalit was the first to enter the drafty clapboard bungalow. Teeth chattering, she called out cheerfully, "Brrrr. It's freezing in here! Where's the switch for the central heating?"

Tzippi smacked the side of her head and guffawed, "Central heating. That's great! Why didn't I think of that?"

The others joined the general frivolity, clapping Margalit on the back and congratulating her for her fine sense of humor. Margalit was puzzled. What had she said that was so funny?

"Pass the hot chocolate and get out the ice skates." Tzippi was really getting in the mood now. "I think I see some *frost* on the window pane!"

The girls tittered as they began to get ready for bed. Margalit got the feeling that she'd better not mention the heating again; seeing the layers of clothing the girls were gathering to wear to sleep, she realized ruefully that this was as warm as the bunkhouse was likely to become.

Although all the other Achva bunkmates had succeeded in completing their unpacking and spreading their linens on their beds, Margalit was still pulling things out of suitcases when it was time for Lights Out. Just when she was about to despair of finding her blanket among all the mounds of clothing Maria had packed for her, she opened her biggest piece of luggage and breathed a deep sigh of relief.

There, nestled in the suitcase, was her electric blanket! And beside it was the sheepskin that belonged between the sheet and mattress! Ruffled sheets and huge thirsty towels made up the rest of the package. Margalit had never felt so relieved in her life.

Arranging her linens was not a big problem in the dark. Margalit just dropped the proper layers on the bed and smoothed each one on top of the other—first the sheepskin, then the bottom sheet, then the top sheet, then the electric blanket. Climbing into her nest, she discovered a slight problem.

"Anyone know where the outlet is around here?" Margalit inquired into the darkness.

"Outlet? What is outlet?" Olga wanted to know.

"You know, the socket."

When she received no reply, she tried again, "Can anyone tell me where the place in the wall is where you put a plug into?"

"Oh, I get it," Tzippi chuckled. "You want to plug in your space heater, right?"

"No."

"Your coffeepot, then," Shalva guessed. "You want to make us all a hot cup of coffee."

All heads turned to the unfamiliar voice coming from the direction of the cot that until now had stood empty—the one furthest from the bathroom and not near any windows. In the shifting shadows of the dark bunkhouse, only the vague outline of a greenish lump was visible.

"What's *your* name? Where'd *you* come from?" Tzippi peered at the new addition to the Achva bunch.

"My name's Shalva and I'm from Toronto," Shalva replied succinctly.

"Nifty! Toronto!" Chumi was impressed. "I never met anybody from South America before."

Shalva rolled her eyes. "Toronto's not in South America! It's in Canada."

Yehudis got out of bed and came to inspect the interesting foreigner. "Canada. Isn't that where moose and polar bears come from?"

Shalva sighed and replied sarcastically, "Absolutely! In fact we keep two moose in the backyard as pets!"

"What do they eat?"

Good grief! What *did* they eat? "Fish," Shalva offered tentatively. "There's a lake back there, too. The moose just help themselves."

The girls listened to every word in awe.

Shalva was appalled. "Look, folks," she explained, embarrassed, "I was only kidding, okay? I think maybe I'm hallucinating a little. Lack of food does that to me, you know."

"You hungry?" Tzippi asked sympathetically.

"I missed supper, didn't I?" Shalva scowled.

"Well, we can fix that," Tzippi offered graciously. She stretched herself to her full height of five feet and announced gaily to one and all, "Hear ye! Hear ye! A collection is hereby being mounted for our dear new bunkmate from the far north, who, unfortunately, missed her supper. All food items are to be deposited on Shalva's bed immediately! Anyone not making a donation is a . . . a . . . Plotzenheimer Polar Bear!"

Feet slapped briskly on the floor as one after another, the girls crept out of bed and felt in the darkness of their cubbies for leftovers from their trip up to camp. Then, groping in the minimal light, they made their way to Shalva's cot and dropped their offerings.

Shalva ravenously eyed the disorderly pile of edibles that was accumulating at her feet. Helping herself to a foil-wrapped sweet, the grateful recipient of Tzippi's charity campaign warmly thanked one and all.

Maybe this camp won't be so bad after all, she reasoned, retreating into the warmth of her bright green sleeping bag.

As the participants in the food drive scuffled back to their own sleeping accommodations, Margalit waited patiently for someone to remember the question that had triggered the revelation of the new camper in the first place. When she realized that no answer would be forthcoming, she decided to jog everyone's memories.

"So what about my electricity, people? I need an outlet so I can plug in my electric blanket!"

The girls were dumbfounded. Margalit's pleas sounded too earnest to be a joke. Quilts and sleeping bags pulled up to their chins, the members of Bunk Achva were speechless, not really comprehending Margalit's predicament.

Just then, Chedva came into the room to check on her charges, who seemed to be too excited from all of the activity on the first day of camp to go to sleep. "Five more minutes and then no more talking," she announced.

"Chedva . . ." Margalit's voice was plaintive. "Can you turn on the light for a sec? I need to find the electric outlet."

"She wants to plug in her electric blanket," Chumi confided.

"You're kidding, right?" chuckled Chedva. "Making fun of your poor, dense old counselor?"

"Uh uh. Why would I make fun of you?" Margalit disagreed anxiously, her teeth beginning to chatter. "I'm freezing."

"Aren't we all?" Libby commiserated. She had never been so cold in her life.

"Yeah, but I really do have an electric blanket," Margalit insisted.

"Okay, that does it," said Chedva. She switched on the light and was amazed to see that Margalit was indeed frantically waving a plug that was attached to her pink blanket.

Rubbing their eyes from the sudden glare, the inhabitants of Bunk Achva shifted their glances from the technological marvel of a blanket to their new bunkmate from Toronto who was placidly munching her way through a bag of corn chips.

Chumi wormed her way out of her quilt and tiptoed over to Margalit's bed, where she reverently fingered the unusual blanket. Chedva motioned impatiently for Chumi to return to her cot as she loped around the bunkhouse, her eyes on the woodwork. Eventually, the perspiring counselor located the electric outlet . . . just beside Shalva's bed.

She glanced down at Shalva and said warmly, "This is no time for extended greetings, but welcome to the bunk." She hesitantly added, "You in the mood of switching bunks? There's no electric source anywhere near Margalit's bed."

"Sure, why not?" Shalva murmured resignedly, screwing her face up and grimacing. She swept her remaining foodstuff into a neat pile atop her sleeping bag and said, "It's been an awfully trying day. Why should I expect the night to be any different?"

Shalva dutifully followed Chedva to her new sleeping quarters, rolling her eyes and yawning loudly all the way. When she was resettled, remorse stabbed at her for her grouchy performance. After all, the girls had gone out of their way to be nice to her. Pitching onto her side, Shalva broadcast her version of an apology.

"I really do appreciate the nosh, folks!" she hollered. "It should sustain me at least until the morning!"

Chedva surveyed the campers tiredly. They all seemed to be settled comfortably at last. She switched off the light in the cabin and swiftly headed for the door.

With the lights off once more, Tzippi was restless. Hoping to shake everyone up a little, she began telling a ghost story in the eeriest voice she could muster.

"Creep. Creep. Something gray and sinister slithered furtively out of the woods at the edge of the camp. Slowly, ever so slowly, it snaked its way through the grass to the shelter of the closest bunkhouse . . ."

All eyes shifted to the back window of the Achva bunkhouse. Through the dusty blinds, the shadowy outlines of gnarled tree limbs crisscrossed in the moonlight, silhouetted against a navy blue sky. Below them, fern fronds waved to and fro in a gusting wind. It was not hard to picture something out there, lurking in the undergrowth. Bunk Achva was, of course, the dwelling situated closest to the woods.

"The creature was slimy and filthy, covered entirely with long, matted gray hair. Puffs of smoke curled upward into the chilly air from every place it touched."

The view through the window was unsettling. The shivering girls watched in fright as wispy tendrils of fog curled menacingly around the bases of the nearby trees.

Tzippi craned her neck so that she could better observe the tale's effects on her bunkmates. Except for Margalit, who was already sound asleep in the warm cocoon of her electric blanket, the others were listening intently, mouths hanging slightly open, to every word she was uttering.

Tzippi smiled to herself. She knew she had a real gift for telling ghost stories. Sometimes she was a little too good, managing to get even herself deliciously frightened.

"Its bony fingers stretched menacingly in front of it, continuously probing the darkness. The gray thing was searching for the cozy little house it had spotted from its lair in the woods. Its hairy paws were groping, reaching for something firm to latch onto. Until now, the creature's fingers had not made contact with anything solid." Tzippi paused for a minute and was gratified to hear a sharp intake of breath from somewhere nearby. Eight pairs of eyes were riveted to Tzippi's cot as she breathlessly continued, "But then . . . then, the being stretched out its hand and felt . . . a *wooden staircase.*"

Libby tried to remember what kind of stairs were attached to the Bunk Achva porch. Were they cement or wood? She recalled that her duffle had gotten snagged on the railing yesterday while she was dragging it into the bunkhouse. The railing was constructed of logs of various sizes. Uh oh. That meant that the stairs were most probably wood as well. She realized that she was shaking. Was it merely from the cold, or was the story beginning to have its desired effect on her?

"Up the stairs the gray thing flowed, its presence leaving a dirty smudge on every step. Slowly, oh so slowly, so it would appear to be only a fleeting shadow to anyone who might chance to be sitting even a few yards away . . ."

All of the girls knew that their O.D. (the counselor on night duty, who was taking Chedva's place) was sitting outside in front of the bunkhouse on a bench, truly only a few yards away.

"The creature spread itself out all over the porch. Like a puddle of spilled milk, it expanded in ever widening circles, so that it became flatter and flatter."

The silence in the bunk was total. Tzippi hugged her knees under her blanket and resumed her normal tone of voice, "Do you folks know *why* it was flattening itself out?"

There was no response. She waited expectantly and sure enough, a ragged little voice eventually asked, "Why?"

Tzippi licked her lips in delight. This was sure to scare the daylights out of them! "Because . . ." Her voice once more took on its whispery, conspiratorial tone. "Because it could feel a *crack* under the bunkhouse door . . ."

All eyes left Tzippi's bunk to fasten on the thin beam of light coming through a now obvious crack beneath their very own bunkhouse door. Blankets and quilts were gathered tightly; almost everyone was shivering by now.

". . . and it wanted to make itself flat enough to be able to squeeze *under* that crack and get inside."

"Hear anything?" Shalva asked, her teeth chattering.

Tzippi ceased her narrative so that the girls could listen attentively. There did indeed seem to be a slight scratching sound coming from outside. Tzippi decided to incorporate this fortuitous occurrence into her story.

"The creature was having a hard time making itself quite flat enough to get under the very thin crack, so it put out its sharp fingernail and started scratching at the door, searching for the handle."

She paused again, letting the fear settle among her friends. In the silence a cricket chirped and was rewarded by an answering chorus of insect sounds. A train whistle blew mournfully, far off in the distance. The scratching, however, appeared to have stopped.

"Gosh, Tzippi," Yaffa breathed. "My heart's pounding so hard it sounds like a locomotive." She clutched at her pajama top for emphasis.

Tzippi smirked happily. This was one of the parts of camp to which she eagerly looked forward all year. No matter which bunk they put her in, she could always count on her storytelling skills to gain herself an audience and almost instant popularity; she had never met anyone who could match her ability to inspire delectable terror in every listener. She decided to keep the tale moving at a healthy pace while she had the advantage of everyone's undivided attention.

"The gray, shaggy thing was leisurely stretching itself, its hand sliding cautiously over the boards of the door, when its clammy finger came in contact with something solid."

"Oh no! The doorknob!" Chumi let out an involuntary shriek.

Her shriek startled Tzippi, who was getting so caught up in

her own story that she was starting to believe it herself. Tzippi let loose with a bloodcurdling scream, which in turn set off a chorus of answering screeches.

The doorknob started to turn. This caused the decibel level in the bunkhouse to rise even higher. Only Margalit, snug in her toasty covers, was oblivious to the veil of terror that had descended on Bunk Achva.

The handle turned, the door swung open, and the scowling face of the O.D. appeared in the doorway.

"Pipe it down, you guys, okay? You sound like a herd of shrieking hyenas!"

"I think I'm about to expire of scaredy-itis," Libby moaned, and the others nodded solemnly in agreement.

"And I'm freezing to death besides," Shalva groaned. "To think that I came all the way from Toronto, practically the land of polar bears, for goodness sake, to perish of frostbite in the Catskill Mountains during the summertime! I'm going to add another nightgown, pajama bottoms and an extra pair of socks to my sleeping gear."

"That's a great idea," several girls agreed, crawling out from under their covers to fetch extra layers of clothing. As they passed Margalit's bed, they gazed longingly at her pink electric blanket.

The occupants of the Achva bunkhouse were finally getting themselves comfortable, fortified as they were by two or even three nightgowns, pajama bottoms or tights and several pairs of socks, when an unmistakable scratching sound could clearly be heard from underneath the bunkhouse.

"I must be dreaming," Tzippi muttered to herself, pinching her arm to see if she could possibly still be awake. The sting of the reddening skin was her answer.

"D-d-d-did you hear that?" she called out into the darkness.

"Aw c'mon, we're all so tired now," Shalva lamented. "Let us get some sleep around here, for goodness sake."

Tzippi scrunched up in her bed and tried desperately to go to sleep. Could it be that her ears were more sensitive than anyone else's in the bunk? Couldn't anybody hear the scratching noises?

Libby was the first to acknowledge that Tzippi's ears were not playing tricks on her. "Tzippi?" she called tentatively in the darkness. "I hear it, too!"

"Me, too!"

"What do you think it could be?"

Under normal circumstances, Tzippi would have picked up the thread of her story, building the terror to new heights. But the truth was, she had succeeded in scaring not only her bunkmates, but herself as well! What had she created, anyway?

"Ooh," she howled. "Something's under the bunkhouse!"

Scratch, scratch, scratch, the noise under the floorboards continued.

"It's the creature's fingernails," wailed Shalva. "I tell you I should have stayed in Toronto. We may be part of the true North, strong and free, but we sure don't have hairy gray things in our basements!"

The yowling in the bunkhouse now sounded as if a whole den of wolves had invaded. Chedva came up the path to the Achva bunkhouse as the O.D. was rising once more from her seat to quiet the tumult.

"Don't bother," she muttered to her replacement for the evening. "I'll take care of it myself."

Chedva stalked onto the porch in a ferocious mood. The first night of camp, and they were at it already! Couldn't a counselor get any peace at all?

"Okay, what's going on in here?" Chedva barked as she came through the door.

There was such a ruckus that no one even heard her.

Chedva cleared her throat and yelled at the top of her lungs, "*I said, what in the world are you guys up to?*"

"There's a creature under the bunkhouse," Libby ventured timidly.

"It's gray and hairy and has scratchy fingernails," Tzippi contributed.

"It's *gray* . . . and *hairy?* . . . and has *scratchy fingernails?*" Chedva repeated slowly, in disbelief.

Several girls nodded vigorously in unison.

"Boy, did they give me a lulu of a bunk this year," Chedva griped. She turned to face the beds of the campers and, in an irritated tone, complained, "Are you guys trying to pull my leg? You know there's nothing under the bunkhouse."

Tzippi put her fingers to her lips and motioned for everyone to be absolutely silent. Instantly, a hush fell over the bunkhouse.

How did she *do* that? Chedva wondered incredulously.

As all ears strained to pick up even the faintest sound, the steady scratching could be heard distinctly. Visions of a shadowy creature slithering in the dark beneath the floor, trying to poke its hairy finger through a crevice in the floorboards, danced in the campers' brains. They shuddered involuntarily.

"What *is* that?" Yaffa inquired nervously.

"Probably nothing," Chedva assured her.

"How do we *know* it's nothing?"

"I can't sleep with a hairy gray thing near my bed!"

"Ooh! I want to go home!"

Chedva was rapidly losing her patience. She grabbed a flashlight and waved it wildly in the air.

"All right," Chedva declared in disgust. "You guys are asking for it. Everyone get a sweater and meet on the porch."

"How come?"

"What for?"

"It's freezing out there!"

"*Out on the porch this instant!*" Chedva boomed. She abruptly turned and headed out the door.

One after another, the girls in Bunk Achva who were still awake grabbed sweaters and jackets and headed out the door. They congregated sleepily on the porch as Chedva, head held high, proceeded to descend the steps, flashlight in hand.

"Now," she announced grandly, "you are all going to watch as your fearless counselor, Chedva Wilheim, shines her flashlight on the loathsome, fearsome creature under the bunkhouse and sends him packing!"

"Hear, hear!" Tzippi applauded cheerily.

The others merely looked on from beneath droopy eyelids and grunted.

Chedva was now standing at the side of the bunkhouse. She aimed her flashlight into the dark depths beneath the bungalow and caught a frightened animal in its beam. The startled skunk streaked past, spraying the horror-stricken counselor with its distinctive aroma. A loud groan could be heard as it hurtled by and vanished into the woods.

CHAPTER FOUR
Bunk Inspection Blues

Chedva had spent a good part of the night soaking in a tub of tomato juice. Although it hadn't *really* been Tzippi's fault (after all, the idea of crawling under the bunkhouse had been totally Chedva's), she felt just a tad guilty about the episode. When Chedva returned to the bunkhouse in the wee hours of the morning, she found a can of lilac-scented talc on her pillow as a peace offering.

The second day at Camp Tehila did not get off to a promising start. Clean-up was not going well, and Chedva's strained nerves were getting frazzled. The old hands already knew the routines, but the newcomers had to be taught the details. Chedva explained the rotation of chores and set up a workshop to demonstrate the fine points of making hospital corners on the beds.

Margalit tried to pay attention to the intricate procedures for correctly making a bed, but her mind kept wandering. She had never even attempted to make a bed before; Maria had always done it for her. But, she reasoned, what could be so hard about tucking a few layers of bedding around a mattress?

She was to find out soon enough. Standing in front of her cot, Margalit poked the ends of the electric blanket under the mattress. Stepping back to survey her handiwork, she noticed that all the other girls were still hard at work. With a critical eye, Margalit had to admit that although the edges of the blanket *were* invisible, they left a lot to be desired in the neatness department. She tried to ignore the sheepskin bunched up under the covers. The surface of the bed looked like a relief map of New York, with the Catskill Mountains protruding proudly in the center.

What's the difference? Margalit shrugged. I'm the one who has to sleep in it!

Besides, there was still the matter of her luggage. The other campers had emptied their bags the previous day. They had hung their dresses neatly in the closet and piled the rest of their possessions tidily in their cubbies. The suitcases and duffles were now piled on the porch, waiting to be put under the bunkhouse for storage. In light of last night's unfortunate occurrence, Chedva prudently asked the maintenance man to handle this chore for her.

Margalit had used all of her allotted space in the closet, her cubby was full, and still her Gucci bags bulged with an assortment of clothing, footwear, toiletries and assorted odds and ends. The clothes she had worn the day before were strewn on the floor, and her purse dangled from the bedpost.

"Bunk inspection in five minutes!" Chedva broadcast the warning from a prone position on her cot. She was still exhausted from her ordeal of the previous night.

"Remember last year there was a prize for getting seven perfect inspections in a row?" Yehudis asked. She had been singing at the top of her lungs, and her bunkmates were relieved that she was taking a break to stand at the side of Chedva's bed and pose a question. "Did you hear if they're giving anything this year?"

Chedva rubbed her eyes. "Oh yeah. They mentioned something at the staff meeting. Seven perfect cleanups and the bunk gets a pizza party."

"Hey, that's not bad!" Tzippi hooted. "Not bad at all!"

Yehudis stood on her bed and made the announcement to the rest of the group. "Didya hear that? Seven perfect cleanups for a pizza party!" Then she jumped down and meticulously rearranged her quilt so that it would lie absolutely straight on her cot.

Preoccupied with their own chores, no one had taken the time to check out how her neighbors were doing. When the score for Bunk Achva was posted that second day of camp, the girls were shocked to discover that they had only merited a meager 7! It didn't take them long, though, to identify the source of the problem.

"Margalit, what's the matter with your bed?" Shalva demanded petulantly.

"Huh?" Margalit was momentarily nonplussed.

Shalva was getting irritated. "You got a *cow* sleeping in there by any chance?"

Margalit felt a hot flush starting to burn across her cheeks. They had thought she was funny yesterday. Maybe she could get away with a little joke.

"No," she returned stoically. "I pasture my sheep in there. It's so cold out here, you never know when you might need the wool to make some extra sweaters."

To reinforce her point, she reached under the lopsided blanket and yanked out her sheepskin, waving it in the air over her head for emphasis.

First an electric blanket and now a sheep pasture! Not to mention a silver stretch limousine and a chauffeur dressed in full uniform! The girls of Bunk Achva did not know quite what to make of Margalit. But her joke at least distracted them, and by the time they were heading out to first activity, the Achva bunch were all chattering gaily.

Lunch was tomato soup, salad and potato latkes. Tzippi couldn't believe the coincidence. She watched in astonishment as Chedva drained her entire bowl. The girls she could understand, maybe, but Chedva?

Tzippi looked into the red depths of her portion. People sometimes told her that she had an overactive imagination, and today she supposed it was probably true. But try as she might, Tzippi couldn't bear to dip her spoon into the contents of her dish. Finally, she could stand it no longer.

"Chedva, what was it that you said you had to sit in all night after you got squirted by the skunk?"

Chedva wrinkled her nose in distaste. "You know. I told you this morning—it was some kind of tomato juice."

Then, realizing that her interrogator was Tzippi, the notorious Tzipporah Laya Zandberg, she added suspiciously, "Why?"

"Oh, nothing. Just because . . ."

Tzippi lifted a spoon of tomato soup, tipped it and let the

red liquid dribble slowly back into her bowl.

"Tomato soup . . . tomato juice . . ." she muttered under her breath just loudly enough for everyone to hear.

Narrowing her eyes, Chedva watched Tzippi fiddling with her soup. She certainly didn't intend to eat it—that was for sure. Finally, Chedva fell into the trap.

"Something wrong with your soup?" she asked.

"Uh, no!" All eyes were now on Tzippi. You could sense that she had something up her sleeve. "I was just wondering . . ."

She balanced her chin on her pointer finger in her best imitation of a thinker. Chatter at the table died down. Tzippi was now the center of attention.

Finally, Chumi couldn't stand the suspense. "Well? What were you wondering?"

"I was wondering . . ." Tzippi said in a melodramatic voice, ". . . what it was exactly that they *did* with that whole bathtub full of tomato juice when they were finished. You know," she continued, a note of mischief in her voice, "how they absolutely *hate* to waste food in this camp."

Shalva was the first to clutch her stomach. She was the only one in the bunk who had actually eaten almost a whole bowl of the warm soup.

Spoons clattered noisily to the table, as one by one the girls of Bunk Achva realized the implications of Tzippi's allegations. Only Olga continued peacefully ladling soup into her mouth, a contented look on her cherubic face.

"Ooooh, that's disgusting!" the girls agreed.

"Tzipporah Laya Zandberg, you're impossible!" Chedva fumed.

"Thank you," Tzippi replied modestly.

At rest hour, Shalva retired to her bed with what she was convinced was food poisoning. Margalit sprawled on her lumpy mattress, despondently eyeing the six partially unpacked designer suitcases on the floor. Chedva had given her until the end of rest hour to empty them and get them stashed out of the way.

The remaining members of Bunk Achva wandered aimlessly around the cabin. Tzippi decided that it was time for the girls to get to know each other better.

"C'mon everyone," Tzippi beckoned. "Gather round into a circle on the floor and we'll play that famous game called 'Let's Get Acquainted.'"

"I never heard of that game before," Chumi commented.

"Of course you didn't," Yehudis giggled. "That's because Tzippi invented it herself when she was eight."

"It's a really good game, though," Yaffa added hurriedly, as she saw a frown beginning to creep across Tzippi's freckled face. "We usually play it during rest hour on the first full day of camp."

"Everyone tells a little about themselves," Yehudis explained. "That way we can all get to know each other better."

"That sounds like a good idea!" Miriam gushed. It was her first time at camp, and she had been feeling kind of shy.

The girls drifted to the middle of the cabin and plopped down on the wooden floor. Tzippi, as usual, started the conversation rolling.

"I guess most of you know all about me already," Tzippi began. "After all, I do have a reputation to live up to!" She arched and wiggled her eyebrows expressively and smirked at the assembled campers. "Old Tzipporah Laya Zandberg, that red-headed terror . . . mischief maker *numero uno . . . and* I play a mean game of *machanayim!*"

When the rest of the girls seemed afflicted by tongue-tie-itis, Tzippi waved her arm and invited, "Step right up. Step right up. Who else would like the great honor of telling us something about herself?"

Miriam raised her hand. "I guess I'll be next," she volunteered bravely, running her fingers through her straight brown hair. "I live in Baltimore, and it's my first time at sleepaway camp. I never realized it was so cold in New York. Next time I'll know to bring my winter parka!"

Yaffa smiled sympathetically. "Hey, I was here last year *and* I live in New York, and I didn't bring a winter jacket either. I don't remember it ever being as cold during the summer as it was last night! I'm not great at sports, but I love to draw."

"Yeah," Yehudis waved her arm and proclaimed proudly, "you should've seen the great scenery Yaffa helped make last year." She winked at Yaffa and then realized that the girls now expected her to say something about herself.

"And I'm Yehudis," she added, "owner of the voice that's the loudest and the greatest!"

That provoked a merry smile on everyone's lips.

"My claim to fame is that I'm the oldest in a family of eight, and the rest are all boys!" Chumi contributed. "I came here to get a little peace and quiet!"

A round of chuckles followed this revelation. Shalva had been listening to the conversation from her bed. Rolling over and moaning loudly, she did not want to be left out.

"The name's Shalva," she whimpered. "I hail from Toronto,

the land of moose and polar bears, as you all know. When I recover from this awful case of food poisoning, I might even learn to like it here. I had a really great time last night, if you don't count the part where I almost came down with frostbite!"

Libby looked around. Most of the other girls had taken their turns. Shyly, she began, "I'm from Miami. It's warmer there in the *winter* than it was here last night! I don't even have a winter parka. I never realized it before, but I sure am glad I don't!"

"Hey, Miami! That's neat!" Yehudis was intrigued. "Isn't there an ocean down there and everything?"

"Uh huh. It's just like in the books. There are waves and seashells and palm trees." Libby was getting just a bit homesick.

"With all that sun and surf you must be a fabulous swimmer!" Tzippi enthused.

"Actually . . ." Libby started to say, but she was interrupted by the irrepressible Tzippi.

"Hey! We can really use a great swimmer in our bunk! There's a water olympics at the end of the trip, and it's always being won by the bigger kids. Can you dive, too?"

"Um . . . Well, to tell the truth . . ."

"Sure you can! Boy, is that a silly question!" Tzippi was so sports-minded that a person with unusual athletic abilities commanded her instant respect. She sauntered over to where Libby was sitting, and threw her arm around her shoulders in a comradely fashion.

"And," she confided gleefully, "wait till you see the trophies they give out!"

The conversation went on to other topics. Libby stared at the bright pink laces of her running shoes and berated herself for not being more forceful.

I *did* try to tell them, she lamented to herself anxiously, but nobody was listening. Now what am I going to do?

At the other end of the bunkhouse, Margalit was faced with a dilemma. Chedva had told her to put away all her stuff, but she hadn't given her a clue as to where it should be stored. Frustrated, she ran her eye over some of the other girls' cubbies. Some were filled to overflowing, but there were a few that had lots of space to spare.

As carefully as she could, she recombined the contents of the emptier cubbies so that two full cubicles were freed up. Then she tried to cram as many of her things as possible into those two emptied areas. It wasn't terrific, but at least it was a start.

Margalit now had three of her six suitcases emptied. She reshuffled the remainder of her possessions and piled them haphazardly under the bed. Relieved to be done with the seemingly insurmountable task, Margalit began dragging her luggage out onto the porch.

As she passed the circle of friends chatting amiably on the floor, Margalit smiled to herself. Everyone in Bunk Achva appeared to be having a really nice time. It wouldn't be long now before she could finally join them!

The discussion had turned to family members. Chumi was telling about the crazy scrapes her brothers had recently gotten into.

"... so there they were up in the tree, and they couldn't get back down. My father had to call the fire department . . ."

Tzippi chortled merrily. This was a story after her own heart. She had two younger brothers who got into even more mischief than she did, and she decided to get her photo album to show the gang some truly funny snapshots. The cozy gathering was suddenly interrupted by a howl of indignation.

Tzippi stomped back to the ring of girls and demanded angrily, "Okay, whose idea of a joke is this?"

She was met by a sea of blank faces.

Tzippi bit her lip and muttered, "Look, maybe I deserved it. I sure play enough practical jokes on the rest of you. But I worked so hard getting everything arranged yesterday."

Buoyant Tzippi looked a little deflated. Her bunkmates stared at her, concerned.

Finally, Miriam ventured timidly, "Tzippi, can you tell us what's the matter?"

For once, Tzippi was rendered speechless. She pointed in great distress to the cubicle in which, just yesterday, she had so meticulously arranged all of her gear. Now, the cubby was occupied by someone else's belongings; her stuff had vanished!

The other residents of Bunk Achva checked out their own cubbies. More tampering was discovered.

"Whose stuff *is* this anyway?" Chumi asked, puzzled, as she pulled a rainbow array of T-shirts from her shelf. The girls looked at each other, and then their eyes all focused on the one person who had been working in the area all rest hour, who was now innocently struggling out the door with her last overnight bag.

Tzippi shook her red curls in annoyance. "That girl really has a warped sense of humor!"

"Look, Tzippi," Miriam consoled in a gentle voice. "You have to admit that sometimes people feel the same way about you."

Tzippi thought that one over. Miriam did have a point. She

decided to go along with the prank and see if maybe there was something funny about it that had eluded her.

Rest hour was almost over by the time Margalit took her place among the others. They shifted to make room for her.

"So Margalit," Tzippi tried to be as jovial as possible under the circumstances, "how's the old sheep pasture?"

"Okay, I guess." Margalit smiled nervously.

Tzippi couldn't help herself. The next words slipped out unbidden and sounded so vehement, so out of character for the normally easygoing camper, that the girls sitting on the floor fidgeted uneasily.

"What were your sheep doing pasturing in my cubbyhole, anyhow?"

Tzippi blushed as she clapped her hand to her mouth. She promised herself that she would remember to think before she spoke next time. In the meantime, the words hung in the air, menacing and unfriendly. Margalit's jaw dropped.

"Look, I'm really sorry," Tzippi apologized almost immediately. "But why'd you do it, Margalit?"

Margalit burst into tears.

Tzippi felt terrible. "Me and my big mouth!" she chastised herself unhappily.

The tears cascaded down Margalit's cheeks for several minutes. No one moved. Not knowing what to do, Tzippi jumped up to bring Margalit a tissue. Taking the tissue gratefully, Margalit blew her nose and explained what had happened.

"I couldn't help it!" she wailed pitifully. "Chedva told me I had to get my things put away, and I really tried. I never should have brought so much, but my parents were out of town, and the maid did all the packing. Your cubbies didn't look so full, and

I didn't think you'd mind . . ." Margalit corrected herself. "That is, I was *hoping* you wouldn't mind. I really should have asked you first, but I couldn't work up the courage." She sniffed and rubbed her red-rimmed eyes. "I'm so very, very sorry!"

An awkward silence fell over the group as the girls tried to think of a way to help out their bunkmate.

"C'mon, you guys," Tzippi urged, trying to repair the damage she had done. "Let's have a pow-wow and decide what to do with Margalit's stuff."

Yaffa remembered something from her experience with the previous year's scenery committee. "You know," she offered, "there's a gigantic attic over the casino. They store all the scenery up there, but there's still loads of room. Margalit can sort out the things she needs just for this week and put the rest back in her suitcases. We can all help her carry them over and stash them up there."

"That's a great idea!" Margalit heaved an immense sigh of relief. It also solved another problem that she had been afraid to bring up. How was she going to explain to her mother about her designer luggage being stored under the dirty bunkhouse? Now it would be safe and sound up in the attic!

Returning to the scene of the crime, Margalit proceeded to dump the contents of her own cubby and of the two pirated cubbies onto the floor. Emptying the cubicles was the easy part. Now she would have to choose a week's worth of essentials. She surveyed the pile of jumbled clothing helplessly.

In the meantime, Tzippi and Yaffa trooped out onto the porch to retrieve Margalit's suitcases. Chedva had been curled up on the bench in front of the bunkhouse, writing a letter. Out of the corner of her eye, she had watched with relief as

Margalit's suitcases had gradually made their way onto the porch one by one. As rest hour was ending, she licked the envelope, stamped and sealed it and was just about to stroll back into the bunkhouse, when she noticed an unnerving development. Margalit's suitcases were retreating back into the bunkhouse, and in the hands of none other than Yaffa and Tzipporah Laya Zandberg!

Chedva was about to call to the girls when she thought better of the idea. Stalking up the stairs like a sleuth in a mystery novel, she decided to apprehend the culprits in the act.

Chedva burst through the bunkhouse door and bellowed in what she hoped was a suitably fearsome tone, "Okay, what's going on around here now?"

She was greeted by a scene very much like the one she had left a whole hour before. Margalit was standing in front of a huge mound of clothing, shoes, toiletries and other assorted articles. Six suitcases (Chedva counted them twice, just to make sure) were in a ring around Margalit's bed, exactly as they had been when rest hour had started.

Maybe I'm getting senile, Chedva worried. How could I have seen the suitcases moving on and off the porch when they've been here the whole time?

Tzippi approached Chedva warily and looked up into her eyes. "Maybe your encounter with that skunk did you more harm than you realize. Why do you think there's something wrong in here?"

Chedva blinked as she gazed shakily around the bunkhouse. Ten innocent pairs of eyes peered back. She shrugged her shoulders helplessly and directed her attention to Margalit.

"Well, it looks like you haven't gotten much done so far,"

she said. "Do you want me to help you?"

"No, everything's under control now," Tzippi assured Chedva hastily.

Chedva was dubious. "How do you know?"

"Oh, it's actually kind of a complicated story," Chumi remarked.

"Is it?" Chedva was interested.

"There was a slight problem in here," Miriam said in a conciliatory tone. "But we worked it out all by ourselves!"

"Yeah," Yehudis agreed proudly. "So if Margalit needs some help, we're all going to help her!"

The girls drifted over to Margalit, who was vainly trying to sort through her belongings. It was not hard to see that she hadn't the faintest idea of what to select for the coming week.

"Rest hour is up in about two minutes," Chedva informed her crew. "If you're going to help her, you'd better get moving at super speed. Mario said the suitcases have to be out of here by tonight."

Nava stepped forward. She had been so quiet until now that her bunkmates had barely noticed her. "Why don't you folks all go on to afternoon activity? I'm a pro at packing! My mother's been sick the last few weeks, so I handled all the packing for the whole family! And I did all the shopping too! I'll help Margalit sort her stuff in no time flat, and we'll join you before anyone even realizes we're missing."

Sighing with relief, the Bunk Achva bunch headed out to their first afternoon activity—arts and crafts. It was still way too cold to go swimming. And true to her word, Nava arrived with Margalit in tow within half an hour.

The suitcases sat in the bunkhouse until just before supper.

As the announcement was made for everyone to gather at the dining hall, and the masses started lining up near the main house, a convoy of suitcases left Bunk Achva in the direction of the casino. By the time supper was being doled out, and the girls of Bunk Achva were taking their seats around their table, the suitcases seemed to have vanished into thin air.

CHAPTER FIVE

Kitchen Capers

Shalva dipped a ladle into the tureen in the center of the table. She surveyed its contents with distaste and deposited about one tablespoon's worth on her plate. The main course at supper tonight had the consistency of applesauce. It was supposed to be something *fleishig*—suppers always were—but try as she might, Shalva could not locate any evidence whatsoever of meat or chicken in the concoction.

"What is this stuff anyway?" Shalva griped as she pushed the minute amount of food around on her plate.

"Oh, it is being very good," Olga commented brightly, heaping another steaming mound on her plate.

"Stew," Tzippi identified the dish. "If you close your eyes when you eat it, it tastes pretty good."

"Stew?" Shalva asked in an incredulous tone of voice. Her eyes widened as she poked the brownish mass with her fork. "Where I come from, stew has these big chunks of meat and lovely round little potatoes and carrots and onions . . ." She licked her lips as memories of her mother's winter stew came to mind, all glazed in brown gravy.

"Yeah, well that's probably all in here too, somewhere," Yehudis supposed. "It's just that at your house, your mother probably uses a proper spoon to stir it with, and here they use a tire iron or something."

Titters greeted this comment. That set Tzippi to thinking of what the stew might have been cooked *in*. It would have had to be something very big to feed the whole camp.

"Penny for your thoughts," Yaffa begged. She had been watching Tzippi's facial expressions changing as she weighed the various options in her mind.

"Laundry tub," Tzippi answered brusquely. She knew that would pique Yaffa's interest.

Yaffa waited patiently for Tzippi to elaborate. Tzippi, of course, maintained her silence, waggling her eyebrows to indicate that she was still busy thinking. By this time, she had attracted the attention of the rest of the girls at the table.

"So why a laundry tub at dinner table?" Olga inquired innocently. Her mouth was full—she was now on her third portion—and the words were a little slurred.

"I was just thinking . . ." An angelic expression spread across Tzippi's freckled face. She cast a glance over her attentive audience, and when she was sure everyone was facing in her direction, she continued, "I was thinking *what* they could use to cook up stew for so many people. A plain old *pot* would be much too small."

"Oh, no! Here she goes again!" Miriam whispered to Libby. "Better finish up quickly before you lose your appetite!"

Libby smiled at Miriam. "It doesn't bother me. I'm so hungry by suppertime that I could eat a whole *horse!*" She corrected herself. "If it were kosher, of course, and since it isn't, I'll have to settle for second best." She scooped another spoon of stew into her mouth.

"What *do* they use?" Yehudis was interested.

"So I was thinking," Tzippi continued, tossing her red curls, "of a laundry tub! You know, those big old metal washtubs in which they used to scrub clothes a long time ago."

Yehudis turned the thought over in her mind. "That's actually not a bad idea, as long as they cleaned it out first. No wonder the stew gets so crushed up! It's made in a *washtub* and stirred with a *tire iron!*" She clutched her sides in mirth and guffawed loudly.

"It sure tastes like it was!" Shalva grumbled to no one in particular.

Tzippi heard Shalva's muttering, and an idea flashed in her brain like a lit-up lightbulb. She sidled over to Shalva's seat and whispered into her ear, "Did you say you were starving, old buddy?"

Shalva puckered up her mouth and clutched her stomach in answer.

"No problem!" Tzippi reassured her. "I know where they keep all the ingredients before they mess them up by cooking them. And while we're grabbing ourselves something to eat, we can check out what it is they *really* use to cook and stir with in the kitchen."

Chedva appeared at Tzippi's side and gently but firmly guided her back to her seat.

Tzippi sat back in her chair and carefully eyed her new

co-conspirator. Shalva had given up chasing the stew around her plate with her spoon. She hadn't touched any of it. Her stomach rumbled; Shalva was positive this was a signal that raw hunger was beginning to gnaw at her insides. A grin slowly blossomed out of her scowl as she joyfully considered the possibilities of Tzippi's offer. Waving her spoon jauntily in the air, Shalva beamed across the table at Tzippi. Tzippi grinned back and winked.

"Okay, gang, five minutes until Lights Out, and I don't want any funny business tonight!" Chedva passed up and down the row of bunks to make sure that everyone had heard her warning. She stopped in front of Tzippi's bunk with an extra piece of advice just for her. "And *no ghost stories!*"

"Certainly not! I wouldn't dream of it!" Tzippi retorted wholeheartedly, nodding her head vigorously in emphasis so that her red curls bounced merrily up and down. She had no intention of keeping anyone up past bedtime tonight. What she had in mind for tonight depended on everyone falling asleep as soon as possible.

Chedva eyed Tzippi with mistrust. She has something else up her sleeve, she suspected. There was something very fishy about the way she agreed to that. Aloud she said, "I'd better not hear about *any* trouble tonight when I get back."

"When you get back?" Tzippi parroted. "Oh no! Not a chance!"

The red-haired camper grinned innocently at Chedva. No, when Chedva would be getting back, peace and quiet would reign in the bunkhouse. Tzippi herself considered it her personal responsibility to make absolutely sure of that. Chedva would be able to go to sleep without a care in the world. Tzippi rubbed her hands together in glee under the covers. It was only *after* Chedva would be sound asleep that her plan could kick into action!

Tzippi's watch alarm went off at midnight. The bunkhouse was pitch black. Rubbing her eyes, Tzippi was momentarily confused. Why had her alarm sounded in the middle of the night? She rolled over and was about to resume her slumber when the cobwebs cleared from her brain and she remembered *the plan*. She was about to tiptoe over to Shalva's bed to wake her up when she was startled by a pitter-pattering on the window.

"Oh, no, it can't be!" Tzippi groaned. But it was. The rain was running down the window in sheets. "Such a good idea, and now it's spoiled!"

Regretfully, she tucked her covers back around her chin and waited for sleep to overtake her. She waited a long time. Noticing that her toes were turning numb from the cold, she slipped out of her bed to snatch an extra pair of woolen socks. Back in bed, she waited some more. Tzippi checked the luminous dial on her watch. It read 1:25. She tossed and turned. Suddenly, she sat bolt upright. Something was different!

Tzippi cocked her ear and listened carefully. The night noises in Bunk Achva seemed to be the same as always. And then she realized what it was. The rain had stopped! Tzippi gleefully hopped out of bed, loped over to Shalva's bunk and shook her by the shoulders.

"Whatsamatter? Whaddayawant?" Shalva mumbled drowsily, her face buried in her pillow.

"The time has come . . . The coast is clear . . . If you wanna raid the kitchen," Tzippi murmured invitingly, "let's get a move on here!"

"Huh?" Shalva's voice was still fuzzy with sleep.

The poetic approach didn't seem to be working, so Tzippi resorted to the one word that she knew would have Shalva on her feet in a jiffy. "*Food!*" she mouthed loudly.

That did it! Shalva's eyes opened wide, and within minutes the girls were standing in the bathroom washing their hands and splashing cold water on their faces.

Looking up from the sink, Tzippi caught sight of Shalva's reflection in the bathroom mirror. She stuffed her fist in her mouth to keep from laughing out loud. Shalva resembled an overstuffed teddy bear rather than a girl about to go out on a kitchen raid. Her bathrobe was straining at the seams, threatening to split at any moment.

"What're you wearing under there?" Tzippi asked, puzzled.

"Hey, I'm a Torontonian, remember? *We* know how to dress in cold weather."

"You're right," Tzippi agreed, "it must be freezing out there now! But what does that have to do with the strange get-up you're wearing?"

"I'm rigged out in layers," Shalva explained patiently, "the way anyone anticipating heading out on an extended mission into the frozen wastelands gears up."

"Huh?"

Shalva spun around so that Tzippi could absorb the full impact of her well-padded sleepwear. "Three sweatshirts and a pajama top, two pairs of tights and a pajama bottom, and four, count 'em, *four* pairs of socks."

Tzippi glanced down at Shalva's feet. Sure enough, her sneakers were about to explode, too.

"Listen, I think I need to make a few additions to my wardrobe before this jaunt," Tzippi decided. "Don't go anywhere. I'll be right back!"

"Where would I go?" Shalva assured Tzippi's retreating figure. "I haven't gotten my bearings yet in this camp. I'd probably get lost and end up in Albany!"

"And to think that I pride myself on being prepared for every eventuality!" Tzippi berated herself as she made her way stealthily to her cubby. "How could I have forgotten how cold it's been this summer? I would have iced up before we even got to our destination!"

Tzippi's bathrobe was bulging alarmingly when she returned. The two friends exchanged looks and giggled.

"I have to hand it to you," Tzippi complimented Shalva. "You're really on the ball!" Exhibiting the famous Tzipporah Laya Zandberg smirk that spelled instant trouble, she beamed. "You and I, we're going to be some team this summer!"

"Whoa, now, old pal," Shalva cautioned. "Let's take this one step at a time. I've never been the type to go on midnight forays without permission before. The only reason I said okay tonight is because you said the target is good old nourishing *food!*"

"Righto," Tzippi agreed, but then she added mischievously, "Wait and see, though. After you've tried it once, it gets easier the second time. And pretty soon, you're an addict, just like me!"

Shalva winced. She'd never pictured herself the troublemaker type before. But truthfully, she'd never grumbled and grouched as much in a whole year as she'd just done in only two days at this tiresome camp. She'd just have to wait and see.

"So are we going to get a move on before dawn, or what?" Shalva said aloud.

"Aye aye, boss!" Tzippi saluted in response.

With utmost care, the two travellers tiptoed past Chedva's bed. Tzippi edged ahead and, at the bunkhouse door, stopped to squirt something on the hinges. Shalva's eyes widened in surprise.

"You thought of everything!" Shalva breathed, impressed.

"When you've gotten into as much mischief as I have," Tzippi confided when they were safely on the other side of the door, "you learn from your mistakes. Last year, we had really rusty hinges on our bunkhouse, and the squeak gave me away the first time I tried to go out for a little midnight stroll. By now, I have a pretty complete kit put together."

Tzippi withdrew a flashlight from the depths of her enormous bathrobe pocket and switched it on.

"I've never seen such a big pocket before! You must have the kitchen sink in there!"

"Not yet," Tzippi laughed. "But after tonight, you never know!" She rummaged in her bottomless pocket and produced a package of jelly beans. "Vitamin pills to give us energy," she winked.

The duo made their way down the path toward the kitchen. Evidence of the recent heavy rainstorm was all about them. They tried to circumvent any trees along the way; neither wanted to be soaked by a cold shower from the dripping leaves.

The kitchen was shrouded in darkness. Massive clouds hung in the sky, blocking any moonlight from filtering through.

"Kind of spooky, huh?" Tzippi mused.

"Let's just get the food and scram!" Shalva begged. "This place gives me the creeps at night!"

Tzippi approached the kitchen door and yanked at it. It refused to yield.

"Locked," Shalva confirmed as she too tried to pull at the unwilling door.

"Sometimes they leave some of the windows open, though," Tzippi recalled. "Wanna have a try at them?"

Shalva gestured to Tzippi. "After you, fearless leader."

Until now, the two girls had stayed pretty much on the paved path between their bunkhouse and the kitchen. Although there had been the occasional puddle, on the whole they had remained reasonably dry. To get to the kitchen windows, however, they had to tramp through ankle-high soaking wet grass and mud.

It took only seconds for Shalva to call the effort off. "We Torontonians know about stuff like hypothermia and frostbite. Take it from me, Tzippi, it's time to turn back. Frozen feet are a definite no-no!" She looked down at her soggy sneakers with a sad expression on her face. "Even if it means abandoning the food!" She heaved a sigh of dejection.

Tzippi was already at the first window. She rattled it impatiently, willing it to open. It was stuck fast.

"C'mon, let's get out of here," Shalva urged.

"Just one more try!" Tzippi hated to see such a pitiful end to what had promised to be a rewarding adventure. She sprinted to the other side of the building. Shalva watched in alarm as she disappeared around the side of the kitchen.

"I really am getting 'cold feet' about this," she muttered

darkly. "In more ways than one." The thoughts of a full stomach that had spurred her onward all night had vanished like mirages in the desert. Now all she felt was cold and miserable.

Tzippi returned to Shalva's side within minutes. She had not had any luck.

"That Pesha Chaya really keeps things locked up tight this year," she announced sadly. The two girls thought about the stolid kitchen aid who continually barred their way into the kitchen for second helpings. "Other summers, there was always at least *one* window open! And," she confided longingly, "there was always some kind of chocolate frosted cake cooling on the counter!"

Shalva ran her tongue over her lips regretfully. The two sodden campers, their bathrobe hems dripping onto their sneakers, made their way wearily back up the path along which they had come.

"Remember," Tzippi warned, "if anyone sees us, put your hands out straight in front of you, squeeze your eyes shut, and make like you're sleepwalking!"

"Sure," Shalva mumbled disconsolately. She just wanted to put her starving self to sleep in her own bed, and the sooner the better.

Tzippi and Shalva made it back to the Achva bunkhouse undiscovered. They tiptoed back to their beds and drowsily stripped off their bathrobes, drenched footgear and socks, which they balled up and kicked under their beds. Then, still clad in their relatively dry sweatshirts, they scooted under their covers and were sound asleep within minutes.

Morning dawned bright, sunny, but still quite cool. The

occupants of Bunk Achva reluctantly climbed out of their warm nests and trudged to the bathroom to wash *negel vasser*. Most of the campers were still bleary-eyed from sleep, so it took a good ten minutes before the initial discovery was made.

"Look," Yehudis exclaimed, as she pointed in awe at the floorboards of the bunkhouse.

"Wow!" Libby marvelled. "Do you think there's anything we can do before Chedva finds out?"

With her talented counselor ears, honed by years of practice, Chedva caught the last three words from the other end of the bunkhouse. She watched with interest as one after another, the girls gravitated toward the spot where Yehudis and Libby had been standing, gesturing to each other and pointing at the floor.

"Looks as if I'd better have a glimpse for myself," Chedva concluded, pulling on her second sock and tiptoeing stealthily across the bunkhouse. She joined the circle of gawking campers without anyone having perceived her presence.

"And look! They're still sleeping!" Nava noticed. "Do you suppose we ought to wake them up?"

Chedva craned her neck to see what everyone was ogling there on the floor. The girls were bunched pretty tightly together. She stood on tiptoes, straining to see over the heads and shoulders in front of her but suddenly lost her balance. Panicking, Chedva grabbed onto the arm of the nearest girl. Nava's eyes widened when she realized who was hanging onto her sweater sleeve.

Frantically pulling at Yehudis's arm to attract her attention, Nava whispered loudly, "It's *her*!"

"Who?" Yehudis turned, her mouth puckered in alarm.

Yaffa jumped directly in front of Chedva, trying to block her view. "Hi, Chedva! Nice morning, isn't it?" she said sweetly.

Chedva sighed mightily. "What's going on here now?"

"Oh, nothing!" Libby reassured her with a big smile. "Look, you're only wearing socks. Why don't you go put your shoes on?" She tried to coax Chedva to move in the direction of her bed.

In the meantime, Yehudis and Yaffa made a beeline for the bathroom to seek out some rags.

"Oh no, you don't!" Chedva protested indignantly. "Everyone's been having a real grand old time contemplating a mysterious something on the floor, and I fully intend to see what it is!"

She lunged to her feet and elbowed her way through the secure chain the campers had formed. Their ranks broke and Chedva primly stepped forward, her eyes fixed suspiciously on the floor. As the source of the mystery appeared in plain view before her, Chedva could feel her breath catching in her throat.

"I should have known something was up," she groaned. "I had a distinct feeling last night that Tzippi had something good and illegal up her sleeve."

For there, on the floorboards of Bunk Achva, was the incriminating evidence for all to see. Two sets of muddy sneakerprints led from the bunkhouse door directly to the beds of Shalva Silverstein and Tzipporah Laya Zandberg!

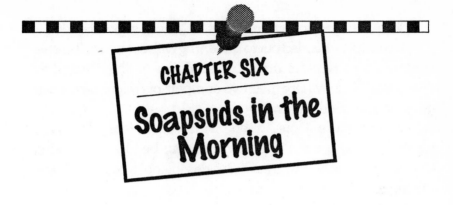

CHAPTER SIX

Soapsuds in the Morning

"**O**kay, gang, stop standing around gawking!" Chedva ordered. "*Shacharis* starts in ten minutes, and it'll probably take you five to get over to the *shul*."

"But what about Tzippi and Shalva?" Yehudis asked in concern. "Shouldn't we be waking them up to come, too?"

"Nope," Chedva replied cheerfully. "Today they get to sleep in."

"Aren't you coming with us?" Yaffa asked in a shrill voice, about two decibels louder than normal. She couldn't understand how the two girls could possibly avoid hearing all the commotion.

"I'll be along later," said Chedva. "Tell Hindy I was unavoidably detained."

The campers moved towards the doorway, shuffling their feet. They dawdled as they were about to exit, peering back into the semi-darkness of the cabin.

Chedva began to get impatient. "C'mon, shoo already!"

Bunk Achva headed out to *davening* without two of its usual contingent of ten. As they strolled down to the *shul*, they speculated about where their two compatriots might have been going in the middle of the night.

"I can't figure it out," Libby lamented to Margalit. "Why would *anyone* get out of their nice warm bed to go traipsing around outside in the mud? Besides being freezing, it was raining, too!"

"Beats me!" Margalit answered, shrugging her shoulders. "I can't stand being in the mud in the daytime!"

"What do you think is going to happen to them?" Chumi worried out loud.

That set into motion a wild set of suppositions. By the time the girls reached the *shul*, they were all filled with nervous anticipation at the fate of their fellows.

Meanwhile, back at the bunkhouse, Chedva had been pondering what, exactly, she ought to do. If the offender had been anyone other than Tzipporah Laya Zandberg, she would most likely have fared better. But Chedva knew all about Tzippi's reputation from years past, and she feared that if she didn't assert her authority early in the season, Tzippi would be doing whatever she pleased all summer long.

Chedva grabbed a chair and positioned it just opposite the head of Tzippi's bed. Then, to pass the time while she was waiting, she began to say some *Tehillim*.

Shalva was the first to stir. She could feel something strange in the air. The sun was streaming in through the windowpane, extending its warm fingers into the dimness of the cabin. And yet, it was awfully quiet . . . uncomfortably, a little *too* quiet.

"Tzippi? You up yet?" Shalva called out.

"Hm?" Tzippi was in the middle of a very pleasant dream, and she clung to the last shreds of sleep tenaciously.

"How about you, Lib?" Shalva tried again.

There was no reply.

"Is everyone still sleeping?" Shalva wondered aloud. She slowly unwound from her covers and sat up in bed. The cots on both sides of her were rumpled but empty. Apprehensively, Shalva swept her gaze over the bunkhouse. As her eyes wandered in the direction of Tzippi's bed, she noted with alarm that *all* the beds except Tzippi's appeared unoccupied.

"What's happening?" Shalva exclaimed. She swung her legs out of bed to investigate more closely, when her attention was arrested by the footprints on the floorboards.

"Uh oh," she whimpered.

As details of the previous night's trek swirled in her brain, Shalva's heart fell into her slippers. Gulping, she squirreled into the relative safety of her covers. When several minutes had gone by, and the lurching of her heart had lessened, Shalva hesitantly poked one eye over the edge of her sleeping bag. She gazed across the cabin at the bed of her still slumbering friend.

There was a chair parked near Tzippi's cot, and to Shalva's horror, there seemed to be something moving on it.

"Tzippi?" Shalva called faintly into the emptiness.

She did not receive an answer. The thing on the chair, though, seemed to be turning in her direction.

"Is there anyone besides Tzippi and me in this cabin?" Shalva cried, addressing herself, in particular, to the being on the chair.

Since no one answered Shalva's feverish calls, she came to

the inescapable conclusion that the thing on the chair was an animal of some sort.

Shalva clutched at her heart. "Where *is* everybody?" she wondered despondently. "And how did that animal get into the bunkhouse?"

Then she realized despairingly that if *no one* was in the bunkhouse besides Tzippi and herself, and if an animal was truly threatening her friend, it would be up to her cowardly self to try and warn Tzippi.

What can I do? she panicked. How can I alert Tzippi without startling the beast?

Desperately trying to come up with a solution, Shalva focused more carefully on the animal to try to determine what sort of creature she was dealing with. The thing twitched, and then suddenly stood up on two legs. Shalva gasped as she realized what, or in this case, *who*, it was!

What should I do now? she wondered, pulling her sleeping bag over her head and waiting for the axe to fall.

Tzippi reached up to scratch her shoulder. Had she been imagining it, or had someone been calling her? Cautiously opening one eye, she peered out from under her snug quilt . . . and had the shock of her life! There, seated placidly on a chair in front of her bed, was Chedva!

"Hi, Chedva," Tzippi grunted shakily. "Something up?" She listened for the usual morning sounds in the bunkhouse, but strain as she might, she couldn't hear a thing.

"Well, *boker tov!*" Chedva greeted her heartily. "Had a very nice sleep now, didn't you?"

"I suppose so. Why?"

"Because you and Shalva are the only ones still in the

bunkhouse," Chedva explained patiently. "Everyone else left for *davening* ages ago."

"Shalva?" Tzippi called uncertainly.

"Uh huh?" came the faint reply from the other side of the bunkhouse.

"Oh." Tzippi gulped. Then she blustered, "So how come no one woke us up?"

"Because you girls must have been *very tired* to have slept right through the Wake-Up bugle."

"Tired?" Tzippi brightened. "Yes, that's it! We were very tired!" She yawned to emphasize her exhaustion.

Shalva listened intently. "She doesn't know about the footprints!" she murmured to herself in distress.

"Well, thanks for letting us sleep in. I guess we'll be getting up now." Tzippi stretched her arms over her head and smiled appreciatively at Chedva.

"No problem!" Chedva agreed. She leaned back in her chair and watched with satisfaction as Tzippi slid out of bed and began to make her way to the bathroom.

"Psst, Tzippi," Shalva whispered anxiously.

"Howdy, Shalva," Tzippi warbled as she went past. "Wasn't that nice of Chedva to let us sleep in because we were so *tired*?" She winked mischievously.

Shalva pointed forlornly to the floor and cleared her throat. "Look down," she said.

"Huh?" The urgent tone in Shalva's voice made Tzippi stop short.

"Just look down on the floor, quick!"

Tzippi gazed at her slippers. "Something wrong with my slippers?"

By this time, Shalva was almost beside herself with suspense at what was going to happen to them. Soundlessly, she pointed to the incriminating evidence. The smile on Tzippi's face faded. The two girls stared at each other in consternation.

"So," Chedva called amiably to the abashed campers, "let's get on with it already. Go wash *negel vasser*, get dressed, and be back here by the time I've finished *davening*! We're going to sit down and have a nice little chat."

Ten minutes later, two very somber campers were perched on the edge of Tzippi's bed, waiting for the interrogation to begin. And begin it did.

"Now," Chedva started out in a friendly enough tone, "can you girls please tell me exactly where you went last night in your muddy sneakers?"

Shalva gulped. "We went outside."

"That is truly a revelation!" Chedva admitted, and then she asked sharply, "*Where* outside?"

Tzippi glanced at Shalva, who had turned a pale shade of parchment white. If anyone was going to ease them out of their predicament, it was certainly not going to be Shalva! Tzippi gathered her wits and confided, "Just past the porch." That was true enough. She didn't bother mentioning how *far* past the porch!

"And what were you doing outside, just past the porch in the *middle of the night*?"

"Breathing!" Shalva squeaked.

"Breathing?" Chedva was incredulous. Even Tzippi's mouth dropped open in astonishment.

Shalva stared at her feet and tried to keep as straight a face as possible. Her foot was shaking, though, and it was making her teeth chatter. "I needed some fresh air," she managed to say.

Chedva turned doubtfully to Tzippi. "And what were *you* doing out there with her?"

"Well, I met her in the bathroom last night . . ." This part was definitely true. "And when she said she needed some fresh air but was afraid to go out by herself, I volunteered to go with her."

Chedva thought that one over. *If* what Shalva was saying was true, it was totally in character for Tzippi to have volunteered to go out with her. Still, her suspicions lingered. Why had both girls been so tired this morning just from going out to get some air?

"Anything else you have to say for yourselves?" Chedva persisted.

Tzippi recognized the element of doubt in Chedva's voice. To quell her skepticism, Tzippi answered with two questions of her own, which she knew would be very powerful food for thought. "It was raining and freezing! Where could we possibly have gone? And why would we have wanted to?"

Shalva and Tzippi held their breath.

"I'm going to go down to the dining room and grab a quick breakfast," Chedva decided. "While I'm there, I'm going to ask around if anything was damaged on the grounds last night, or if mysterious figures were seen in places other than their bunkhouses. You girls get out your *siddurim* and *daven* in the meantime. I'll be back soon with some breakfast for you, and we'll finish our little talk then."

True to her word, Chedva returned, bearing a breakfast tray of eggs and hot cereal, just as Shalva and Tzippi were putting their *siddurim* away. They eyed her expectantly.

"You girls are in luck," Chedva sighed. She had the feeling that there was more to this story than met the eye, but she had no way to prove it. "Everything on campus is still shipshape. So, after you finish breakfast, I'm going to issue the two of you a mop and bucket, and you can get to work cleaning these muddy footprints."

Spooning egg into her mouth, Tzippi contemplated the punishment. Not bad, she reasoned, not bad at all! Shalva had really come through! And everything she'd said was actually true . . . sort of.

Chedva found some laundry detergent and filled the pail with a soapy mixture while the girls were eating their breakfasts. Then, balancing their emptied breakfast trays on her shoulder, she bid them a cheerful adieu, with the admonishment, "Remember, when we all get back from breakfast, there'd better not be any evidence whatsoever of footprints on that floor."

"Oh, no! We'll take care of it!" Tzippi assured her. She picked up the mop and saluted smartly.

As soon as Chedva was gone, the two culprits got down to work. They had the footprints wiped away in no time, and there was still a whole bucket of warm, sudsy water left to experiment with.

Shalva brought her muddy sneakers out from under her bed. "Gross, huh?" She flinched, holding her nose in disgust.

"No problem!" Tzippi chirped brightly. She went to fetch her own mud-caked running shoes. "We'll wash them!"

"Great idea!" Shalva dipped one sneaker into the soapsuds and happily watched the mud run off the shoe and into the water.

"Wait a minute! You're getting the water all dirty!"

"So?"

"So let's wash the rest of the stuff we tossed under our beds yesterday and then do the sneaks."

"Hey," Tzippi marvelled when the last sock emerged from its bath clean and fresh. "Just like the laundry tubs of yore!"

Shalva smirked. "Remember yesterday, when you convinced everyone in the bunk that their food was being cooked in a washtub and stirred with a tire iron?"

"Hm?"

"Yeah, well *now* it makes sense to me. You neglected to mention that the cook was washing her clothes first and forgot to empty the water before she dumped in the stew ingredients!"

"Oh, that is truly nauseating!" Tzippi sniffed. "I sort of liked the taste, in an odd sort of way."

"Well, now can I do my other sneaker?"

"Sure."

Tzippi attended to her own messy footgear while Shalva went to hang the soggy socks on the clothesline behind the bunkhouse. Then Tzippi brought all four sparkling running shoes out onto the porch and laid them out to dry.

The campgrounds were still deserted. Tzippi could hear the strains of *Birchas Hamazon* drifting up from the dining hall.

"Let's go back in and see what else needs washing," Tzippi suggested. "We don't have too much time left."

She swung the door open exuberantly, and the force knocked over the pail of soapsuds, which had been standing just inside the doorway. With sinking hearts, the girls watched the river of light brown bubbly water spread like a massive stain over the floorboards.

"Now look what we've gone and done," Shalva wailed. "Chedva's gonna think we did it on purpose!" She dragged the mop through the river.

"That's it!" Tzippi brightened, pointing enthusiastically at the moving mop. "We'll wash the whole floor!"

Giggling, the duo set to work.

When the Bunk Achva bunch made their way hesitantly back to the bunkhouse, after a suspenseful breakfast with their two bunkmates still missing, they were greeted by an astonishing sight.

There, hanging from the porch railing by their laces, were two drenched but clean Keds and a pair of equally soggy Nikes. And attached to the door with a wad of bubble gum (there hadn't been scotch tape in the bunkhouse) was a hand-lettered sign: CAUTION! WET FLOOR!

Clean-up was under way. Tzippi and Shalva strutted around like proud peacocks.

"With such a clean floor, we're sure to get a 10 today!" Shalva could already taste the warm stringy cheese and crisp crust of the pizza.

Yehudis was at her cubby straightening up. "Not if you don't make your bed, we won't," she called across the room.

"Oh, right. Thanks for reminding me!" Shalva bustled over to fix her bed.

"So where'd you guys go last night?" Libby whispered as she passed Tzippi's cot.

"State secret," Tzippi informed her gaily. Then, seeing Libby's face fall, she added comfortingly, "Nowhere really. It turned out to be too cold and wet."

Libby nodded. It was just as she'd thought. Then she asked in a small voice, "Can I come with you next time?" For she was sure, as the rest of them were, that of course, there *would* be a next time.

"Sure, kiddo." Tzippi smiled benevolently. "I'll put you on my list. The more, the merrier."

Libby grinned as she returned to her bed to plump her pillow. Beside her, Margalit was wrestling with her covers, trying mightily to get the layers to lie flat. Just as she thought the corners were tucked in perfectly, the sheepskin got loose and lumped up in the middle of the bed. Margalit stared despairingly at the odd sight; it looked like a sick camel was lying in her cot, with its humps pointing straight up in the air.

Start again, Margalit told herself. She tried to stay calm as she mentally issued directions. First, she pulled on the edges of the linens in an effort to tame them. When that didn't work, she flopped down on the mattress and tried to shove the lumps to the side of the bed. Finally, deciding that the situation was utterly hopeless, Margalit grabbed the sheepskin by a wooly curl and yanked it out of the mess. Now she could make some headway with the sheets and blankets!

When the bunk inspector arrived, Margalit joined the others, confident that this time she had not let them down. The sick camel was gone from her bed, and in its place was a reasonably flat electric blanket, tucked in carefully at all the crucial places.

Everything was going smoothly until the bunk inspector got to Margalit's bed and tripped over the sheepskin, which Margalit had dropped on the floor and forgotten about.

From her prone position on the floor (very clean, she had

noted), the bunk inspector asked through clenched teeth, "What *is* this?"

"My rug?" Margalit croaked in a tiny little voice.

"Well, see to it that this rug is rolled up and put away! It's much too dangerous!"

"Okay."

The bunk inspector painfully made her way to her feet and glanced down irritably at Margalit's bed. "And those aren't proper hospital corners," she observed.

Limping over to the big chart posted on the cabin wall, the bunk inspector pencilled in a bold red 8.

Margalit glumly stared down at her running shoes. She felt just awful. No one had said anything nasty to her this time. But she was positive that everyone was secretly hating her all the same.

The sun was shining brightly in the sky, but it was still much too cold for a morning swim. First activity for Bunk Achva was changed from swimming to *machanayim*.

Reactions to the substitution were mixed. Tzippi rejoiced; *machanayim* was, after all, her very favorite sport. Shalva sulked; to her, any sport was bad news. Libby was so pleased with the switch that her face was almost swallowed up in an ear-to-ear grin.

On the way to the *machanayim* court, the girls discussed their extraordinary morning. Although Tzippi and Shalva were not eager to elaborate on their midnight foray, they were only too pleased to give a blow-by-blow account of what had occurred in the bunkhouse from the moment they had opened their eyes.

"It was so quiet, I thought maybe Camp Tehila was a bad dream and I was waking up in my own peaceful bedroom at home," Shalva started dreamily. "My own stereo, my four poster bed with its ruffled canopy, my . . ."

Tzippi cleared her throat loudly.

"Oh, sorry!" Shalva apologized. "I guess I was just getting carried away with happy memories. Anyway, I realized within a few minutes that almost all of you had already left . . ."

"We *tried* to wake you up," Yehudis explained.

"We were talking at the top of our lungs!" Yaffa added. "We couldn't believe you didn't hear us!"

"We must have really gotten knocked out from that damp, freezing night air," Tzippi rationalized. She was pleased to hear that her friends had not totally abandoned the guilty two.

"It was kind of scary being all alone in the bunkhouse," Shalva continued in a quavery voice, shivering at the memory. "But then I saw something that made my skin prickle and my hair stand on end!"

"Hey, I'd better watch out," Tzippi remarked. "You're almost as good at telling spooky stories as I am." Then, accusingly, she added, "You didn't tell me this part!"

"Sh," Miriam hushed her sternly. "So you'll hear it *now* with the rest of us."

The bunch edged so close to Shalva that she had a hard time keeping from tripping over their feet.

"So what were you seeing?" Olga queried, her enormous eyes even rounder than usual.

"It was perched on a chair right near Tzippi's bed, and it was *moving* . . ." Shalva squeezed her eyes shut, remembering her utter terror.

"Ooh," Libby breathed shakily. "I would have been scared out of my wits!"

The others bobbed their heads in agreement.

"What *was* it?" Nava begged. "Hurry, tell us!"

"I thought it was some kind of creature from the woods," Shalva confided. "But then it stood up, and it only had two legs!"

Tzippi burst out laughing. The rest of the gang scowled.

"You're spoiling the story!" Margalit accused. Then she clapped her hand to her mouth and tried to blend back into the background.

"What's with her?" Yaffa whispered, noticing Margalit's odd behavior.

Nava, who had noticed Margalit's strange actions too, shrugged her shoulders.

"So, already what is happening?" Olga was beside herself with curiosity.

"So the thing stood up on its two legs, and I realized it was . . . Chedva!"

"No kidding!"

"What was Chedva doing there?"

"I would have jumped out of my skin!"

"Yeah," Tzippi picked up the thread of the story. "When I opened my eyes, the first thing I saw was our dear counselor. But I couldn't figure out what she was doing there."

"She wished Tzippi a *boker tov*," Shalva continued, "and told her that everyone was long gone. Would you believe Tzippi actually thanked Chedva for her great consideration in keeping us company?" Shalva chuckled, and Tzippi blushed.

"That was before I knew about the hard evidence," Tzippi explained.

By this time, the group had arrived at the *machanayim* court. Most would have been content to spend the entire activity period listening to the tales the two offenders had been spinning. But this was, after all, *machanayim*, and Tzippi was not to be deprived of even a minute of it.

"To be continued at lunch," Tzippi promised as she lurched onto the court with a ball.

Teams were being chosen. Shalva edged away from the action. Foot by foot, she was getting closer and closer to the bushes that rimmed the court, when a hand grabbed her by the collar and nudged her back onto the playing field.

"You'll be sorry!" Shalva warned. "I've got two left feet when it comes to most sports, and *machanayim's* just about my worst."

"Don't be silly," Yaffa admonished. As evidence of her faith in Shalva, she picked her for her team.

The field was soon filled with the wild cries of the two teams. Tzippi was at her usual best, swerving and swooping to avoid oncoming balls and then, just when the opposing team thought they were about to hit her, she whirled and grabbed the ball, sending it back into play for her side.

True to her word, Shalva was back in the bushes, legitimately this time, within minutes of the start of the game. She was the first one to be knocked out of play.

Margalit was on the team challenging Tzippi's powerhouse squad. She surprised everyone by her graceful evasive actions and magnificent catches. When the activity was over, she was one of the four girls who had not yet been struck out of play.

Tzippi was the most surprised of all. She sidled over to Margalit and enthusiastically punched her on the arm. "You never told us you were so good at *machanayim!*"

Margalit rubbed her arm and grinned shyly. "I didn't know!" she said happily.

"Whaddaya mean you didn't know? You must be one of the first ones chosen when your class plays at school." Tzippi had never heard of a school in which *machanayim* was not the favored recess activity.

"Actually, *machanayim's* not the hottest sport in our school. Basketball's the biggie! We have a fabulous gym and a real team!" Margalit's eyes flashed proudly. "I've seen *machanayim* played occasionally, but today was absolutely the first time that I've tried it myself!"

Tzippi stared at Margalit in disbelief.

"And I had a really fun time." Margalit swung her long black hair over her shoulder, and her smile widened. "Maybe all those ballet and gymnastic lessons helped out."

"Boy," Tzippi muttered under her breath. "If she's that good her first time out, imagine how great she's gonna be with practice."

As the Achva bunch sauntered off to their next activity, Tzippi lagged slightly behind, trying to digest the information she had just discovered.

Lucky I'm not the jealous type, she tried to reassure herself.

"**B**ECAUSE OF THE COLD WEATHER, SWIMMING ACTIVITIES THIS AFTERNOON WILL BE CANCELED. ALL BUNKS SCHEDULED FOR SWIMMING, EITHER FIRST OR SECOND ACTIVITY, WILL BE GOING ON A HEALTHY HIKE! HIKERS ARE TO REPORT TO THE HANDBALL COURT AFTER REST HOUR FOR WARM-UPS!"

"Aw." Yaffa was disappointed. "No swimming again!"

"Not unless you brought a wet suit and frog flippers," Yehudis chuckled. "Ever hear of anyone going swimming in a winter coat?"

"I'd chance it," Shalva offered. "At least you don't need much energy for swimming. You can just lie on your back and drift around the shallow water. To go on a hike, you need *lots* of energy. Energy comes from a steady supply of good, nourishing food . . ."

"Yes," Olga joined the conversation belatedly, "very good

food for lunch, I am thinking. The fish was being special delicious!"

Shalva rolled her eyes. Oh, was that fish? She smiled sweetly. "I couldn't tell *what* it was."

"Oh, yes. Very fish!" Olga nodded her head emphatically. "I was having maybe four or five."

Libby was sitting cross-legged on the floor, writing a letter on her new lilac-scented stationery. Relief had flooded over her in waves with the announcement that swimming was being canceled. She would gladly have agreed to hike twenty miles rather than face the gang now at the swimming pool. Libby scanned what she had written so far.

> Dear Abba and Ima,
>   Brrrrrr!
>   The geography books have it all wrong. New York can't possibly be in the United States. It must be located somewhere near the North Pole! Last night it was so cold at night activity that we had a contest to see who could make the biggest cloud with their breath. One of the girls in our bunk, Tzippi, claimed that her clouds couldn't compete because her nostrils were already frozen together!
>   I was pretty worried on the flight, but you were right—someone did meet me at the airport, and we had a really lively ride up to camp, clapping and singing the whole way.
>   The bunkhouses don't look anything like I imagined. They're made out of wood, kind of like the log cabins Abraham Lincoln must have lived in (and

probably just as drafty!).

The best word for the food here is *interesting*. Although it usually has the texture of mush, it tastes pretty good. One of the girls (Tzippi again—she's very funny!) claims that the reason it looks like that is because they cook it in a washtub and stir it with a tire iron. Isn't that a riot?

There are nine kids in my bunk besides me. We're a regular international mix—Shalva's from Toronto, Miriam's from Baltimore, Nava and Chumi are from Monsey, Olga's from Russia (but now she lives in the Bronx), Margalit's from Long Island, Yaffa's from Flatbush and Tzippi and Yehudis are from Boro Park. They seem like a real nice bunch.

Some of the kids here are under the mistaken impression that just because I come from Miami, with all its sun and surf, I must be a fantastic swimmer. Boy are they going to be surprised when they see that I can barely tread water!

Libby winced as she read the last paragraph. She'd better work up her courage to tell everyone the truth before it was too late. She fervently hoped that the opportunity would present itself while the girls were hiking.

Today's too cold for swimming. We're going to have a hike instead.

Regards to Mindy and Chaim.

Love and kisses,
Libby

Carefully folding the letter in thirds, Libby slipped it into its matching lilac-scented envelope as Nava crouched down beside her.

"Poor Libby," Nava sympathized, clucking her tongue. "You must be really upset that it's too cold to go swimming!"

"Who, me?" Libby squeaked. She mentally kicked herself. Here was her chance to put everything right, and she'd muffed it again! Determined to explain everything once and for all, Libby was just about to open her mouth when Yehudis bounded over.

"Hey, Lib," Yehudis queried, a look of intense interest on her face. "How many laps do you usually do in a day?"

Swimming was one of Yehudis's favorite activities, and she was fairly good at it. But, living in the city, she didn't get the opportunity to practice very often. The idea that someone might be able to do laps every day intrigued her.

"She swims *every* day?" Margalit was impressed. There was a swimming pool, surrounded by tropical plants, in the basement of the Rothman residence, but Margalit only used it a few times a week.

"Sure!" Yaffa piped up. "Wouldn't you, if the ocean were right around the corner from your house?" She crooked her arms and swung them over her head in her finest imitation of a front crawl.

"Hold on a minute," Libby protested. "The ocean's not right around the corner from my house."

"It isn't?"

"Nope! You actually have to walk a couple of blocks to get there."

"Oh, pardon me!" Yaffa corrected herself obligingly.

"Wouldn't you if you lived a *couple of blocks* from the ocean?"

The girls chuckled. Around the corner, a couple of blocks, what difference did it make? Most of them had never even *seen* the ocean.

"What is it being like, this ocean?" asked Olga. She plopped down beside Libby, smiling encouragingly.

"Well, on a calm day, the ocean is kind of bluish-green, with little ripples of white foam," Libby began dreamily. "The waves run up on the sand pretty slowly, and they bring with them small shells, little rocks and other stuff like that. The water is *very* salty. Most of the year it's nice and warm . . ." Libby was getting homesick again.

"And on not calm days?" Chumi prompted.

Libby pondered. "Well, right after the summer is *hurricane* season . . ."

"Ooh!" Chumi sucked in her breath.

Olga widened her eyes. Whatever a hurricane was, it sounded awfully interesting. "I am not knowing this word," she said apologetically.

"It's a big storm," Margalit explained.

"Lots of rain," Shalva added. "And howling winds!" She rounded her mouth and gave her best imitation of a Canadian timber wolf.

"Is sounding very scary," Olga whispered, shuddering.

"Oh, it can get really scary, all right!" Libby concurred.

Tzippi rocked back and forth on her heels in her excitement. "So tell us about it already!" she urged.

"During hurricane season," Libby recounted, "it pours all the time." She glanced across the room at Shalva, who was readying herself for another wolf impersonation, and giggled.

"And the winds howl even louder than Shalva and her four hundred Canadian moose."

"Timber wolves," Shalva corrected immediately.

"Fair enough," Libby continued agreeably. "Louder than Shalva and her four hundred Canadian timber wolves."

Shalva shook her head and mumbled in a peeved voice, "Imagine confusing moose with timber wolves!" But everyone was so interested in Libby's story that Shalva's words went unnoticed.

"With all that wind and rain, the ocean must be wild!" Miriam burst out.

"Well, the waves are enormous! And they crash onto the beach! Sometimes, when it gets really stormy, the water comes right onto the streets, so that it looks like the ocean is lapping at the buildings." Libby paused to catch her breath. "The waves bring all sorts of strange things with them: boots and tires and rusty tin cans and car parts. After the storms, we go out treasure hunting. There are loads of gross seaweed and driftwood, but sometimes you can find really neat seashells. Once we found a birdcage in pretty good shape."

"Wow!" Chumi gazed in awe at Libby. While Libby had been describing the details of a hurricane in Florida, Chumi had been remembering the conversation that had prompted the story in the first place. Having a bunkmate who was a great swimmer was terribly tempting to her.

"Listen," Chumi appealed to Libby as the girls were digesting the details of what it was like to be caught in a raging hurricane. "I don't swim very well." She coughed and scrutinized Libby through downcast eyes. "Actually, I can't swim at all. Do you think that maybe you could give me some pointers?"

Libby grinned. At last! "I'm awfully honored," she beamed. "But the truth is, I don't swim very well myself. I could use some pointers too!" There. She'd said it.

Tzippi edged closer to Libby and punched her arm playfully. "Oh, don't be so modest. Be a good sport and give old Chumi some tips. You were once a beginner yourself!"

Libby was dumbfounded. She'd finally worked up the courage to set things straight, and no one had believed her! What was she going to do?

"REST HOUR IS NOW OVER. ALL HIKERS, LACE UP YOUR RUNNING SHOES AND SCOOT ON OVER TO THE HANDBALL COURT FOR WARM-UPS. EVERYBODY ELSE PROCEED TO FIRST ACTIVITY."

In the mad rush for sweatshirts and sneakers (everyone had been so involved with Libby's story that they had forgotten to ready their gear), the discussion about Miami and swimming was all but forgotten. Only Libby continued to mull over the entire dialogue as the girls raced out of the bunkhouse, bound for the handball court.

"I've never heard of warm-ups for a hike," Yehudis commented as they approached the large cement slab that was the handball court.

Tzippi had been jogging slightly ahead of the others. She turned and confided, "Oh, I heard they've got a new sports counselor this year."

Tzippi always heard all the news first, especially if it had anything to do with sports.

"She's supposed to be a real professional," Tzippi said seriously. "I think she coached a school's soccer team in Israel."

"Soccer?" Shalva shuddered. "Ugh!" Now *that* was a sport she was sure she'd be awful in, and she'd never even played it before.

"*Bevakasha!*" A thunderous voice bellowed from the front of the handball court.

All eyes turned in amazement to the short but sturdy teenager standing there. A chorus of murmurs swirled through the air.

"When I say *bevakasha*, this means I want everybody to be quiet!" To reiterate her point, the young lady bounced up and down and blew a powerful blast on the whistle hanging from a chain around her neck.

The murmurs died. Feet shifted uncomfortably, waiting for the next instructions.

"Now, we warm up the muscles. I do each exercise one time by myself. Everyone watches. Quietly! Then everyone follows and I count. Like so! *Bevakasha!* Neck warm-ups!"

The counselor tipped her neck to her right. Then she pivoted it backwards, to the left and finally, tucked her chin against her sweatshirt. This was greeted by some titters. The counselor was not amused.

"So. Perhaps I am funny? Who thinks I am funny?"

The handball court was filled with rows of silent about-to-be-hikers.

"Who thinks I am funny will come up here and do ten push-ups."

Tzippi considered it briefly, but decided to wait a while and see what else was in store.

"*Bevakasha!* Neck warm-ups! And one and two and three . . ."

It looked like an army boot camp. Rows upon rows of campers dutifully rolled their necks in time to the count of the drill sergeant.

"*Bevakasha!* Arm circles!"

"*Bevakasha!* Toe touches!"

"*Bevakasha!* Lunges!"

"And one and two and three . . ."

Shalva was rapidly becoming fatigued. How am I going to go on a hike? she worried. I'm not even going to be able to stand up by the time this torture is over! Still, leery of the public push-ups in front of the whole camp, she tried to keep up with the exercises as well as she could.

"*Bevakasha!* Back stretches!"

The drill sergeant arched her back. Moans and groans were heard as the campers tried to imitate her. Suddenly, Tzippi poked Shalva. Shalva rubbed her back and jabbed Yaffa. Yaffa stared in amazement and prodded Chumi. Chumi motioned to Olga and Nava.

The object of their attention was positioned on the handball court with her hands and feet touching the ground, stomach pointing up in the air. Her whole body was arched into a perfect semi-circle. As the count continued, Margalit uncurled her back, as natural as you please, and stood back up.

"How'd you *do* that?" Tzippi burst out, astounded.

There was a roar from the front of the ball court. "You in the red hair! Please to come up here and show us how to do some push-ups!"

Tzippi made her way to the place indicated and performed ten faultless push-ups. Even the battle-axe sports counselor was impressed. Smiling, Tzippi skipped back to join her group.

After a few more minutes, the stretches were finally over. The now limber campers gathered in knots to await their counselors and begin the hike. The members of Bunk Achva circled Margalit deferentially.

"Arch your back again," Yehudis begged.

Obligingly, Margalit stretched her arms way over her head, arched her back and bent so far backwards, that she finally touched the ground with the palms of her hands. She was thrilled that she was, at last, an object of admiration rather than scorn.

Yehudis gaped. "Where'd you learn how to *do* that?"

"I take gymnastic lessons," Margalit replied proudly. "We always do a few of these during warm-ups. They're called bridges or limbers. There's other neat stuff I can do too, but I can't show you here because it wouldn't be *tzniusdik*."

"Like what?" Tzippi was intrigued.

"Oh, things like back walkovers and front walkovers and handsprings."

"Huh?"

"A back walkover is sort of like what I just did, but instead of standing back up, you kick your foot over your head and then stand up on it."

The girls exchanged wide-eyed glances.

"Show us tonight in the bunkhouse," they begged eagerly.

Before Margalit had a chance to respond, there was another thunderous announcement from the front of the handball court.

"All bunks are to line up behind their counselors and march out to the road. And one and two and . . ."

Eager to leave the premises before the sports counselor reminded herself that she had left out some crucial exercise, the girls scurried to obey. Within minutes, neat lines of girls in pairs were traipsing down the driveway toward the road.

"I can't move another centimeter," Shalva complained to Libby as she hobbled beside her.

"A what?"

"A centimeter!"

"I never heard of that muscle before."

"A centimeter's not a muscle. It's a metric measurement."

Libby was stumped. "Sorry. You'll have to clue me in. I never heard of that stuff either."

Shalva was puzzled. "Well what do you use to tell you how long this is?" She lifted her two pointer fingers and spaced them about a centimeter apart.

"Let's see." Libby examined the distance. "Half an inch."

"Well, in Canada that would be a centimeter!"

Libby smiled. "Oh, now I get it. I must be a real moose brain!" She giggled.

Deterred only momentarily by this minor delay, Shalva returned to her whining. "So anyhow, if I have to go another half an inch, I think I'm going to faint."

"Oh, don't be silly," Libby reassured her nervously. Because of Shalva's foot-dragging, they were already the last on the line and getting progressively further from the nearest pair.

"I'm getting dizzy," Shalva warned.

"Okay, so lean on me."

Draping her arm reluctantly around Libby's shoulder, Shalva staggered for a short time at her side. Libby watched in despair as Nava and Chumi, the next-to-last pair in line, disappeared over the crest of a hill.

"Can't you walk any faster?" Libby urged. "We're going to get lost!"

"Are you kidding?" Shalva panted. "I'm moving at super speed here. My tank's running totally on empty. I haven't had good solid food for a couple of days now."

"Oh," said Libby, praying that Chedva would eventually notice that the two of them were missing.

In the meantime, she tried to change the subject, hoping that Shalva would forget about scary stuff like fainting. What would Libby do if Shalva really *did* faint and there was no one around to help her? It was not especially cold, but Libby was shivering.

"So, what's your favorite activity in camp?" Libby asked. She was attempting to keep Shalva alert and on the move.

Her answer provided Libby with little comfort.

"Sleeping!" Shalva grunted, trying to maintain an erect posture.

Libby tried again. "Wasn't last night's night activity fun?" she asked, in what she hoped was a cheerful tone. "I thought we'd never capture the flag!"

Shalva was too busy giving her weary feet instructions to answer. "Now left foot move and step on ground. Now right foot move and step on ground. Now left foot. Now right. Left. Right."

"Is something the matter, Shalva?"

Libby was getting worried. Her consternation increased dramatically when she glanced in Shalva's direction to see why she was so quiet. Shalva had turned as pale as a ghost. She *is* going to faint! Libby panicked.

"Help!" she screamed.

Jolted by the abrupt screech, Shalva stopped in alarm, teetering precariously on her feet.

"Sit down," Libby advised her staggering friend in apprehension.

She eased Shalva into a sitting position. They were now sprawled on the side of the road all by themselves, with cars whirring past and trucks rumbling by.

"I don't think anyone can hear us over the traffic sounds," said Libby. She scrutinized the empty ribbon of roadway ahead. "We'll just have to sit tight until somebody notices we're gone."

"You're such a pal," Shalva mumbled gratefully.

Libby was stubbing the toe of her sneaker into the soft red earth of the road shoulder, when she heard a commotion up ahead. Exhaling in relief, she thought it was the finest sound she had ever heard. Sure enough, the eight members of Bunk Achva, with Chedva in the lead, were heading back to retrieve the two absentees.

Chedva was embarrassed. What would Hindy say about a counselor losing two of her crew along a busy road?

To cover her discomfort, Chedva strode purposefully up to the two campers lolling at the side of the road and scolded, "What's the big idea? You can't just sit down and rest wherever you feel like it when we're on a hike!"

"It's my fault," Shalva grimaced. "I thought I was about to faint from starvation."

"She was as white as a sheet and could hardly walk," Libby volunteered. "I called for help, but none of you could hear me over the sounds of the traffic. So I pulled Shalva down. I figured you'd notice we were missing and eventually come and rescue us."

"Libby's a hero," Shalva whispered through chapped lips.

Tzippi had been the first of the Achva campers to reach the stranded duo. She was just in time to catch Shalva's protest that she had been weak from lack of food. Unslinging her canteen from her belt, Tzippi graciously offered it to Shalva.

Tilting her head back, Shalva took a swig of the ice-cold water inside. She swallowed it gratefully and croaked, "I'm starting to feel better already."

"It was a good idea to bring a canteen," Chedva commended Tzippi. "I'll have to remember that for next time."

"That's me," Tzippi crowed proudly, "Tzipporah Laya, Prepared-for-Anything Zandberg!" To Shalva, she added, "It's part of my mess kit, you know. Wait till you see what else I have!"

"We're only a short distance from our destination, the new Jewish library that just opened up," Chedva said. "When we arrived and regrouped, we noticed you were missing. Think you can make it?"

"Sure she can!" Tzippi threw Shalva's arm over her muscular shoulder and pulled her gently to her feet. As she was bending down, Tzippi put her mouth to Shalva's ear and murmured, "We have plans to discuss, you and I."

"We do?" Shalva gasped in surprise.

She hobbled obligingly beside Tzippi as the rest of the girls admiringly circled Libby. Chattering excitedly, the group made their way back up the road several hundred yards to the library.

"Now we're going to stop here for half an hour," Chedva explained as the knot of girls entered the building. "There are books on the shelves and periodicals on the racks. If you want, you can just sit around on the floor cushions and relax. Those of you who need to, can use the bathroom facilities. We'll regroup in the lobby at," she glanced at her watch, "precisely three-thirty camp time."

The girls jostled each other playfully and then split up. Libby headed straight to the special section which carried a full complement of Red Cross safety publications. She was looking for books about swimming.

Maybe I can find something with pictures that will give me some hints, she hoped fervently. She pulled out several volumes and settled down on a cushion to browse through them.

Most of the other girls clustered in the area where the latest Jewish magazines were displayed. Soon they were happily thumbing through articles on everything from fashion to fiction, from world news to gourmet cooking.

As soon as everyone appeared occupied, Tzippi jabbed Shalva in the arm and, trying to remain inconspicuous, the two girls made their way down the hall leading to the bathroom.

"Why are we going to the bathroom?" Shalva asked, puzzled.

Tzippi put her finger to her lips and smiled. Motioning with her head for Shalva to follow her, she cruised right past the bathroom door and continued down the hallway. Pausing only long enough to ensure that Shalva was indeed behind her, she gracefully turned the corner and walked briskly until she reached the library's back door. As Shalva breathlessly drew near, Tzippi swung the door open and guided her friend through.

Shalva peered uneasily around. "Where are we going?" she asked, confused.

"Shalva, old buddy of mine, we're going to play a quick game of I Spy. Know how to play?"

"Sure. But . . ."

"No buts. We don't have much time. Just take a look across the road and tell me what you see."

Shalva sighed. "Oh, okay. I spy with my little eye . . . a gas station."

"That's fine! Now keep going."

"I feel silly."

Tzippi scowled. "Listen, I'm doing this for you. You want to come along or not?"

Shalva stared at her shoelaces. "I suppose," she answered unenthusiastically. She continued with the game. "I spy with my little eye . . . a pet store . . . a laundromat . . . a ShopRite . . ."

"Well?" Tzippi pranced around, grinning.

"Sorry. I don't get it," Shalva apologized. What was Tzippi getting at, anyway?

Tzippi reached her hand into the pocket of her denim skirt. "You didn't ask me what else I had in my mess kit. But," she announced benevolently, "I'm going to show you anyhow." She withdrew her hand from her pocket and, with a flourish, waved a five dollar bill in the air. "Ta Dum! Tzipporah Laya Prepared-for-Anything Zandberg has a stash of cash!"

"So?"

"So, my uncomprehending friend, I am going to lend you this money so you can obtain for yourself some good, healthy *food!*" She pointed grandly to the supermarket across the street.

Shalva's eyes opened wide as she comprehended exactly what Tzippi had in mind. Excitedly, she squeezed Tzippi's hand, and a sunny grin spread across her face.

"Well, what are we waiting for?" she shouted. "Let's go!"

Holding hands, Shalva and Tzippi raced across the road and bustled happily into the ShopRite. Shalva scanned the aisles in ecstasy.

"What should I get?" she wondered aloud.

"Just remember that all I have is five bucks, and that has to include tax."

Making their way down the aisles, Shalva selected an item, then returned to replace it when she found a better choice. Eventually, she had collected a bag of bagel chips, three nectarines, a banana, a small package of kosher cheese and a tiny can of tuna. Mentally tallying the total, she was relieved to see that she had not exceeded the budget. Hugging her acquisitions to her sweatshirt, Shalva was suddenly overtaken by a wave of guilt.

"Don't you want something for yourself?"

"Not today, old buddy!" Tzippi beamed. "Today you need it more than me. I'm glad to be of service."

In a jolly mood, the duo made their way to the checkout counter. Tzippi consulted her reliable watch.

"Listen, we're starting to run out of time. Head for the Express Checkout."

Shalva dutifully traipsed over to the first register and deposited her groceries on the counter. She waited patiently as the cashier rang in the purchases of the little old lady in front of her.

"Now wait just a minute," the stooped woman complained. "You rang in seventy-nine cents for the lettuce. The sign clearly said the lettuce was only fifty-nine cents."

"Listen, lady," the cashier arrogantly popped her gum. "I ring in a number for the vegetables, not a price. The computer says the lettuce is seventy-nine cents!"

"I want to see the manager!" the woman shouted loudly.

Shalva rolled her eyes in exasperation. "Now what?" she asked Tzippi in panic.

They had only minutes to spare to get back to the library on time. All of the other registers had several people in line, and each person's cart was brimming with groceries. Shalva clung to her carefully selected foodstuff, unable to bear being parted from it.

The haggling was still going on when Tzippi suddenly appeared at Shalva's side and dragged her to a register that was miraculously just opening. Relieved, Shalva transferred her things to the empty counter and was checked out in the nick of time. Tzippi politely asked for an extra bag as they were about to leave.

"Okay. Now here's what we have to do," Tzippi explained as the two girls dashed madly across the road towards the library. "You take the groceries and tuck them under your sweatshirt. I'll take the fruit." She reached into Shalva's bag and withdrew the nectarines and banana, dumping them unceremoniously into the bag she was carrying. "These need special care, and I'm more experienced."

Tzippi concealed the fruit in the folds of her sweater, as the friends made their way back down the hallway towards the bathroom. Just as they were approaching the bathroom door, Chedva appeared at the other end of the hallway.

"You're late," she griped. "Everyone's waiting out front."

Tzippi and Shalva exchanged glances. Then they shuffled out to meet the rest of the group, careful not to move suddenly and rustle their bags.

"Where were you?" Yehudis inquired as the girls paired off for the return trip. "I didn't see you in the bathroom."

"We stepped out for a minute for some air," Tzippi explained cheerfully. The "air" excuse had served them well once before; might as well take advantage of it again.

Satisfied, Yehudis moved off to join her partner. Shalva and Tzippi brought up the rear of the line, but they were careful to stick fairly close to the rest of the Achva bunch. They carried on a loud and lively conversation all the way back to camp in order to disguise the unmistakable crackling of cellophane coming from the folds of their clothing.

CHAPTER EIGHT
Cascading Currents

Shalva snuggled into her sleeping bag, a banana in one hand and a nectarine in the other. She smiled dreamily as nectarine juice dripped unnoticed down her chin.

There was an unnatural stillness hanging over the Achva bunkhouse this evening. Ten exhausted campers were lying sprawled across their beds or tucked cozily into their covers, and Chedva had not even given her customary five minute warning before Lights Out.

"Ooh! I've got zigzagitis in my zambizoids!" Tzippi complained, flexing her leg muscles.

"Me too!" Yaffa exclaimed. "And I never even knew I *had* zambizoids until today!" She massaged the cramp in her leg and smiled wryly.

Tzippi eased her aching body out of her cot. She crawled laboriously across the bunkhouse and plopped down beside Shalva's bed. Eyes squeezed shut in bliss, Shalva was so preoccupied with her evening snack of fresh fruit that she was totally oblivious to Tzippi's arrival.

"Ahem . . ." Tzippi loudly cleared her throat.

There was no immediate response from the lump under the bright green sleeping bag. Suddenly, Shalva stretched out her arm and dropped a banana peel . . . right onto Tzippi's red curls.

"Yech!" Tzippi sprang up, howling in protest.

"Eek!" Shalva screeched in terror. Tzippi had bounced up at her side like a giant human jumping jack.

Shalva's scream triggered an answering chorus of alarm from the rest of the Bunk Achva crew. This, in turn, brought Chedva racing in from the bathroom, where she had been placidly washing her hair.

"Now what?" she begged, raising her eyes heavenward, her sopping wet hair dripping down the back of her model's coat.

From the doorway of the bathroom, Chedva's eyes swiftly scanned the cabin. All of the girls appeared to be in their beds, fatigued from their afternoon trek and trying to alleviate the pain from their sore, aching limbs. No, that was not quite accurate. All of the girls—*except one*—were draped across their beds. There was one cot, rumpled bedding notwithstanding, that was not occupied. That was, of course, the sleeping quarters of a camper by the name of Tzipporah Laya Zandberg.

"Okay, Tzipporah Laya, come out, come out wherever you are," Chedva called resignedly.

Tzippi's sheepish face appeared beside Shalva's bed. She waved companionably to Chedva. The banana peel was still on her head.

"I give up." Chedva was too tired tonight to expend much energy on arguing. "Why are you wearing a banana peel?"

Tzippi gingerly reached up and removed the offensive article. She pinched her nose with one hand and handed the peel to Shalva with the other.

"I do believe this is yours," she said politely.

Shalva clutched at her lurching heart. Her breath came in spurts as she dutifully accepted the banana peel back.

"What were you doing down there?" she screeched. "You frightened me half to death!"

Displaying a suitably aggrieved expression, Tzippi replied sedately, "Is this the way you treat someone who has come to fulfill the *mitzvah* of *bikur cholim*? By throwing a banana peel on her head?"

"Let me get this straight. You were fulfilling the *mitzvah* of *bikur cholim*. Here in the bunkhouse. Just before bedtime." Chedva spoke slowly and clearly, carefully enunciating every word.

"Right!" Tzippi nodded vigorously, her red curls bobbing merrily.

"And who, exactly, were you visiting?" Chedva was perplexed.

"Why, my pal Shalva, of course," Tzippi replied. "To see how she was feeling after almost fainting today on the hike." She smiled piously.

"Okay, *rebbetzin*, you have five minutes in which to visit," Chedva warned, "and then it's Lights Out!" She turned on her heel and was almost at the bathroom when an odd thought struck her. Funny, I haven't seen any bananas in the dining room since camp began, she realized.

A sudden desire for a banana overtook her. She spun around, sending rivulets of water in all directions, and called to

Shalva, "Next time they have bananas for dessert, save me one too, okay?"

Shalva and Tzippi exchanged amused glances. "Next time they serve bananas around here, we'll save you one for sure," Tzippi promised solemnly. Shalva nibbled at the inside of her cheek to keep from cracking up.

The two girls maintained their silence until they were sure they could hear the water running in the bathroom sink. Then they collapsed in fits of giggles.

"Just make sure you keep the cheese out of sight," Tzippi cautioned, stifling a chuckle. "That may be a little harder to explain."

"No can do, oh fearless leader," Shalva apologized.

"Why not?"

"Cause I finished it off before supper!" Shalva grinned impishly. Then, with a wink, she added, "Together with the bagel chips, of course."

"How did you manage to eat supper, then?" asked Tzippi. "Weren't you too full?"

"The bagel chips and cheese *was* supper! You didn't expect me to eat that brown mushy thing they served, did you?"

"For your information, that 'brown mushy thing' was meatloaf. And it was kind of good, in a strange sort of way." Tzippi licked her lips, remembering. "The mashed potatoes weren't half bad either."

Shalva wrinkled her nose in distaste but then brightened. "Listen, that was the best supper I've had since I got here. Thanks, Tzippi!"

"Much obliged." Tzippi snickered. She twirled gaily and curtsied, then headed back towards her bed, calling over her shoulder, "I see my *bikur cholim*'s done you a world of good! You're sounding much healthier already."

As Tzippi was getting herself comfortable in her nest of covers, Chedva reappeared with a towel swathing her head and switched off the lights.

"What a roller coaster of a day!" Margalit mumbled gloomily into her pillow. She had gone from mortal embarrassment to pleasure, and then from ecstasy to depression, all in the space of about twelve hours.

Margalit cradled her soft, ruffly pillow in her arms as she mulled over the events that had triggered her emotional highs and dismal lows. First there had been the funny footprints in the morning. Margalit grinned as she remembered the expression on Chedva's face when she'd caught sight of the muddy tracks. Of course they had ended up leading straight to the bed of that irrepressible redhead, Tzippi!

The gang had spent a good part of the morning guessing at the consequences, but no one had been quite prepared for the cheerful reception they had received at the bunkhouse after breakfast. The two offenders had been positively beaming, the floor was spotless, and everyone had attacked clean-up, positive that this was the day they'd get a sure start on that pizza party.

Margalit cringed as the details of the inspection came to mind. She squeezed her pillow in frustration as she recalled the awful ignominy of being the cause of the bunk's puny score at clean-up—again—despite her best efforts. She had felt really dejected. A black cloud of melancholy had settled over her head. She just *knew* that everyone in Bunk Achva secretly hated her.

Then she had played a pretty respectable game of *machanayim*, and popular Tzippi had actually given her a compliment! That had felt really fine. The nasty black cloud had shifted, and its shadow moved slowly away.

Then, at warm-ups for the hike, the highlight of her day had occurred. Recollecting, Margalit gave her pillow a fierce hug. Following instructions, Margalit had done a perfectly ordinary backbend. In her gym club in Long Island, everyone did them routinely. But here at Camp Tehila, it appeared to be a really unique thing. The group had been so impressed that they had asked her to give them a demonstration in the evening.

All during the hike, while her partner Yehudis had been occupied singing loudly to herself, Margalit had been choreographing a short gymnastic routine in her mind. Over and over, she had replayed the moves until she was perfectly content with the results. At the library, Margalit closed her eyes and searched her memory for some fancy dance steps to hold the whole thing together—a cat leap here, a stork stand there.

By suppertime, Margalit was so excited, she could hardly swallow her food. She visualized the great thrill the girls would derive from her little show; why, they'd probably all want her to give them gymnastic lessons at rest hour! And she'd be so happy to oblige. She could form a mini gym club. She'd ask Albert to get badges made up and everything!

Night activity had finally ended. The foot-weary members of Bunk Achva had dragged themselves into their cabin and hastily prepared for bed. Yawning loudly, they had climbed under their covers, forgetting their recent admiration of Margalit's gymnastic prowess. Now the lights were out, and the opportunity to show off her moves was lost. Margalit stared dispiritedly at her crumpled pillow. She had released all her frustrations on it, but she didn't feel any better at all! Tossing and turning, Margalit futilely tried to fall asleep to forget her bitter disappointment.

Libby stared at her nails in the dark. They were bitten to the quick. Nailbiting was a bad habit she thought she'd left behind years ago.

"It must be this swimming business," Libby reasoned glumly.

Lately, her nerves were constantly on edge whenever anything having to do with swimming was mentioned. And to think that she'd actually been looking forward to swimming in a pool instead of the salty old ocean! How had she gotten into this fix anyway? And, even worse, how was she ever going to get out of it without totally disgracing herself?

Libby tucked the edge of her quilt under her chin and closed her eyes. She could hear Margalit thrashing around under her electric blanket.

"Now there," Libby supposed, with just a twinge of jealousy, "lies a girl who has no problems at all! She's got suitcases full of clothes, she's pretty and she's good at all kinds of sports because she gets all the lessons she needs. I bet if I had swimming lessons, I wouldn't be in the pickle I'm in now."

Libby screwed up her eyes and waited for sleep to overtake her. The slow, measured breathing of her slumbering bunkmates was calming, but it was not quite calming enough to lull her to sleep.

"I'll count sheep," she decided. "One sheep, two sheep, three sheep . . ."

Images of fluffy white sheep jumping over a rickety old fence danced in her brain. "Two hundred and seven sheep . . . two hundred and eight sheep . . ."

As Libby was getting more and more exhausted, and despairing of ever falling asleep before morning, a strange thing began to happen to the pictures of the sheep in her mind. The white sheep were turning into frothy white waves, rolling placidly on a calm ocean. The logs from the fence were disintegrating and being swept away by the lively waves.

Libby tried to focus on the thick brown logs, to discern what was happening to them. While her attention was thus diverted, the calm wave tips began foaming up. The water became choppier, sending the logs hurtling down what was rapidly becoming a wide river with white tinged rapids. The logs began crashing into each other as the raging river became wilder and wilder.

Then, on one of the logs, Libby noticed something different. Struggling to make it out, she realized that it was a little animal, hanging on for dear life! Without thinking, Libby dived into the swirling waters, hoping to rescue the cute little creature.

Up ahead the water seemed to flow straight into the sky! Curiously, Libby watched several of the logs further ahead reaching the mysterious void and disappearing from view. All of a sudden it hit her with frightening clarity. Those logs weren't flowing into the sky. They were dropping over a waterfall!

Libby was making good progress toward the animal when the most horrible realization dawned on her. She couldn't swim! Buffeted by the cascading currents, Libby desperately tried to keep her head above water.

"Help!" she screamed in terror. There was no answer save for the thundering of rushing water.

The waterfall was looming closer and closer. Libby faced a dreadful fate. Either she would disappear in one of the whirlpools all around her, or she would be carried over the waterfall and dashed on the jagged rocks below. There was nothing to grab onto.

Wait! There, up ahead in the water, was a skinny branch. If she could only get a hold of it, she could save herself!

Libby reached for the elusive little branch. It danced just out of her reach. The roaring of the water was so loud in her ears, she thought her eardrums might burst.

Libby stretched with all her might. The scrawny branch brushed the tips of her fingers and sprang away. She would only have one more chance before she was swept away to her doom! With a supreme effort, Libby extended her arm as far as it would go and grabbed for the branch.

She must have missed because, without warning, Libby felt herself falling. She must have been swept over the waterfall! She landed with a thud. Carefully running her hands over her body, Libby checked for broken limbs. No, she must have landed on something soft—she seemed to be all in one piece, although one thigh seemed slightly sore. She didn't feel wet, but she could still hear water running.

Cautiously, Libby opened one eye. To her shock, she was lying atop her quilt on the floor beside her bed.

"Then it was all just a dream," she sighed in relief. Funny, though, she could still hear water running.

With a start, Libby realized that her arms and legs were becoming numb from the nippy air. Tossing her sheet and quilt back onto her cot, she was just about to clamber into the heap when she noticed a ray of light peeping from beneath the bathroom door. Tilting her head, she could clearly hear the sound of rushing water coming from the bathroom.

Someone must have left the shower running, Libby theorized. Then another thought struck her, and she raced for the bathroom. Chedva had been washing her hair. What if she had forgotten to turn off the faucet?

Easing the door open slowly, in case a flood of water was waiting on the other side, Libby peeked into the bathroom. No, the sink faucets were all closed.

Sighing with relief, Libby stepped into the bathroom and groped for the shower, squinting against the sudden light.

"I'll just turn off the water and get back to bed," she proposed to herself groggily. Suddenly, she tripped over something soft and furry.

Terrified, Libby's voice froze in her throat. She opened her eyes wide, and met the steady gaze of Margalit, who was squatting at the base of the shower, clad in a fuzzy bathrobe and slippers.

"What are *you* doing here?" Libby croaked, her heart still pounding wildly in her chest, like a bucking bronco at a rodeo.

"Sitting," Margalit replied simply.

Libby was puzzled. "Was it you who turned the shower on?" she asked. The water was still going full force, but Margalit sure didn't look like she was about to take a shower.

Margalit's eyes were downcast as she answered softly, "Yes, it was me."

"Oh." Libby started backing out of the bathroom, shaking her head. Was this something New Yorkers did in the middle of the night—sitting on the bathroom floor, contemplating a running shower? It was certainly not familiar to *her*!

As she was shuffling back to bed, Libby paused and scratched her head. Something had been peculiar in that bathroom, that was for sure. She shook her head, trying to clear it of the cobwebs of slumber. Then, startled, Libby realized what had been wrong.

Abruptly, she turned and retraced her steps to the bathroom. The entire time they had been talking, Margalit had kept her head lowered, but for an instant the two girls' eyes had met. And Margalit's eyes had been all red, as if she'd been crying!

Libby poked her head tentatively back into the bathroom. Margalit hadn't moved, and the shower was still running. "Want some company?" Libby offered.

Margalit raised her red-rimmed eyes and nodded her head in the affirmative. "I guess so."

"What's the matter?" Libby asked in concern.

Margalit sniffed loudly. "I was just crying, that's all. I put the shower on so nobody would hear me."

"Oh." Libby didn't want to be intrusive. She wondered what she should do now. The two girls sat in companionable silence.

"You homesick? I am, a little, myself," Libby admitted.

"No, that's not it," Margalit answered sadly. "If I were really homesick, I would just go home. Actually, I kind of like it here."

"Oh." Libby felt positively moronic. Was this the only word in her vocabulary? In the middle of the night, she just couldn't think straight.

Rubbing her eyes, Margalit peered at Libby from under her long black lashes. "Do you hate me?"

"Huh?" Libby was not sure she had heard correctly. "Could you repeat that please?"

"I *said*," Margalit patiently repeated, "do you *hate* me?"

"Why in the world should anybody hate you?" Libby was astounded. "What'd you do?"

"You know."

"I do?" Libby gazed innocently at Margalit.

Margalit calmly stared back, her big blue eyes filled with misery.

"I mean," Libby corrected herself, "I don't!"

"You don't know, or you don't hate me?"

"Both!"

"I *know* everybody hates me!" Margalit wailed.

Libby caught herself just as she was about to ask, again, why anybody should hate Margalit. At this rate, they could go on in circles all night.

If only Tzippi were here, Libby thought to herself desperately, she'd know what to do. Frantically, Libby tried to figure out how the easygoing redhead would react to the current situation.

First, she'd throw her arm around Margalit's shoulder, Libby realized. Libby was about to extend her arm, but that really wasn't her style. Instead, she dropped down on the floor beside Margalit and said earnestly, "Honestly, I think we're all getting along great together. Whatever the matter is, I'm sure it's not as dreadful as you think."

"But it *is* dreadful," Margalit bawled wretchedly. "Everybody was so excited about the pizza party, especially poor Shalva, who says she's wasting away of malnutrition. They all work so hard at cleaning up to get a perfect 10.

"And *every* day things are just hunky-dory until the inspector gets to *my* bed. No matter how hard I try, there's always something horribly wrong with it. I'll *never* get it right!" Margalit wrung her hands in anguish. "I can tell that everybody wishes I would just pack my bags and go back home."

Libby stared at the tips of her striped socks. She was not overly fond of pizza, but a party was, after all, a party. She herself had been kind of annoyed at Margalit for being so sloppy and ruining their chances. Imagine how someone like Shalva must feel, desperate as she was for store-bought food!

Nobody had mentioned anything about the pathetic bed-making to Margalit. But their feelings must have been awfully obvious to the distraught girl. Libby felt absolutely terrible, and she knew the rest of the girls would be mortified, too if they knew how they had hurt Margalit.

"Tell you what we'll do," Libby murmured encouragingly as she reached into the shower to turn it off.

Margalit looked at her blankly.

"We're going to have a private bed-making class right now," Libby said. "Hospital corners aren't hard to do if you know a couple of tricks. I was having trouble with them myself until Yehudis kindly showed me what I was doing wrong."

"Really? You think you could teach me how to do them?" A tiny flash of hope played over Margalit's troubled face.

"Sure!" Libby exuded confidence. In reality, she was vaguely uneasy about her generous offer. Libby herself had only just learned to make the pesky corners two days ago.

Margalit struggled to her feet and followed Libby out of the bathroom. "So what do I do?" she whispered.

"You have a flashlight?"

A faint smile played at the corners of Margalit's mouth, and then a full-fledged grin broke through. Now here was something she could indeed provide.

"Let's see," she chuckled. "Do you want the penlight flashlight, the regular all-purpose handheld variety, the floating lantern or the deluxe halogen edition with flashing red lights for emergencies?"

"Is there one that you can stand on the floor so that it shines on the bed?"

"Yup. Be right back."

For the next fifteen minutes, Libby and Margalit practiced the fine art of making hospital corners on Margalit's electric blanket.

"I do believe I've got it!" Margalit finally chirped in her best British accent.

"That's great!" Libby heaved an immense sigh of relief. She was afraid she was turning into a solid block of ice.

"Thanks loads, Libby," Margalit whispered as she crawled into the folds of her toasty coverlet. "Anytime *you* have a problem, be sure to come to me first."

Libby galloped back to her cot and dove under her quilt. When she was all settled in and comfortable, she had a brainstorm.

"Margalit, you know how to swim?" she called hopefully across the bunkhouse.

Unfortunately, Margalit was so exhausted from the trying events of the day that she had fallen into a deep sleep the instant her head had hit her ruffled pillow.

CHAPTER NINE

Victory in Sight

"**M**oan. Groan. Ech. Feh." Tzippi rolled over and drew her cover back over her head.

All around the Achva bunkhouse, the reactions of the awakening campers were similar.

"Ow!" Yehudis wailed. "My legs are on strike." She pulled herself to a sitting position and regarded her legs with concern.

"Your legs?" Yaffa goaned. "My whole body's shut down!"

"No problem. Dr. Zandberg can prescribe the perfect solution for all of your afflictions!" Tzippi's voice was muffled by her blanket. She withdrew her head for the punch line. Sore as she might be, this opening was too good to resist. "*Bevakasha!*" she bellowed at the top of her lungs. "Body curlups! And one and two and three . . ."

Chedva burst out laughing. That Tzipporah Laya was a handful, all right, but she had just the right all-purpose remark for any occasion!

Olga was the first to sling her towel over her shoulder and head for the bathroom. Her bunkmates eyed her in awe.

"No aches and pains this morning?" Chumi called in disbelief as Olga sauntered jauntily by.

Olga stopped and stared at Chumi. "Why pain?" she asked, bewildered.

"From the hike yesterday, remember?"

"You be having pain?" Olga was genuinely concerned.

Chumi raised her arm weakly, and it fell heavily back onto the blanket with a thud. She repeated the procedure with her other arm and was about to start on her legs, when Olga graciously inquired, "You want I be going and calling the nurse?"

"No, I'll be okay," Chumi responded feebly. "Don't worry!"

Olga scrutinized Chumi curiously, then shrugged her shoulders and continued on to the bathroom. After all, when they finished *davening*, breakfast would be waiting, and she didn't want to be late.

Tzippi digested Olga's remark about sending for the nurse as she gingerly attempted to maneuver her creaking joints out of bed. She had not been to the infirmary yet this year. Was today the right time to pay the nurse her first visit?

It all depends what they've got on the schedule for morning activities, she decided. Just in case the schedule was not to her liking, she assumed an exaggerated hobble on her way to the bathroom to wash *negel vasser*.

"What's the matter with your leg?" Shalva queried as Tzippi lurched past.

"Oh, I'm not sure yet," Tzippi chortled. "But just in case the injury is severe enough to merit a visit to the infirmary later, I'll let you know in case you want to accompany me."

"Sure thing!" Shalva agreed eagerly. She jumped out of bed and slipped her feet into her slippers. It sounded like an interesting day was shaping up and, fortified by the energizing food from yesterday, she was anxious to be a participant.

On her way to select a T-shirt from her cubby, Shalva paused to listen to the sounds of a Bunk Achva morning. Yehudis was singing her very own rendition of the new Mordechai Ben David song they kept playing over the Camp Tehila P.A. (if not for the familiar words, it would have been hard to guess exactly what it was she was singing). Water was running in the bathroom as ten girls made a run on three sinks. Slippers were slapping against the floorboards as feet ran back and forth to the closet and the cubbies, and then they were joined by the thudding of running shoes as their already dressed owners scampered out the door.

"C'mon girls, hurry it up!" Chedva called from the front porch. "It's pretty warm out this morning. There's a good chance we'll be able to go swimming today."

Libby had been cautiously easing her throbbing thigh out from under the folds of her quilt when Chedva had broadcast her weather report to a wildly cheering bunk. She slunk back under her covers and groaned.

"What's the matter, Libby? Do you feel charley-horsed?" Margalit appeared beside Libby's bed, fully dressed. "I learned how to massage sore muscles at the gym. Want me to rub down any place special?"

Yeah, Libby felt like saying. I need someone to rub down my brain! How could I have let things get to the point where even when I tell people the truth, they don't believe me? And then maybe someone could work some magic on my jaws, so that when I finally summon up the courage, my mouth will slide open real easily and tell everyone loud and clear that *I don't know how to swim!*

Aloud, though, Libby said simply, "Thanks for the offer, but I don't actually feel all that bad. We do a lot of walking on the boardwalk back home, and I must be in better shape than I realized."

It was not Libby's muscles that were the source of her discomfort. It was the black and blue mark on her thigh, from her unfortunate tumble over the "waterfall" and onto her quilt on the floor, that was causing her distress. And how could she possibly explain that?

Libby stretched her arms way up above her head and winked at Margalit. "I guess I'm just a wee bit tired from last night," she murmured.

"I woke up extra early this morning," Margalit confided excitedly. "I've been practicing those tricks you showed me, and I think I've finally gotten the hang of tucking in the corners the right way!" A radiant smile illuminated Margalit's face, and her bright blue eyes crinkled with pleasure.

"That's great!" Libby gave Margalit the thumbs-up sign as she flung her quilt to the side and gingerly slid her legs out of the bed.

Waving gaily, Margalit turned and headed for the bunk-house door, her long shining hair swinging around her shoulders. Watching Margalit's retreating back, Libby pondered all of the things that had passed between the two girls since the previous night.

And to think that only a few hours ago, I was lying in bed

thinking how fantastically lucky Margalit was, Libby marvelled. If I could have chosen any girl in the bunk to switch places with, it would have been her. And yet, outward appearances can be so deceiving! Who would have dreamed that Margalit was hiding all that misery under her cool, calm and collected designer clothes?

Shaking her head in wonder, Libby limped to the bathroom to ready herself for *davening*.

On the way back to the bunkhouse after breakfast, Shalva noticed that Tzippi's leg appeared to have made a miraculous recovery.

"What happened to your . . . ahem . . . *severe* injury?" Shalva snickered. She sidled up to Tzippi and jabbed her playfully in the side.

"Are you kidding? Did you see what the morning activities are?" Tzippi widened her eyes and grinned good-naturedly at her pal. "Swimming and volleyball!"

"How's someone with a mortal wound on her leg going to play volleyball?" Shalva inquired in mock concern.

"No problem!" Tzippi responded almost instantaneously. "The same way someone who was about to expire of hunger and thirst yesterday managed to sprint across the street on the way to ShopRite."

Shalva blushed. "Did I really manage to sprint?"

"Yes indeed! We all have these magical restorative powers we don't even know about. Besides," Tzippi whispered conspiratorially, "someday we're going to need that trip to the infirmary much more than we need it today. It only works well once. After that, there are all kinds of hassles."

Shalva nodded in understanding. The duo joined the other members of Bunk Achva who were slowly straggling into the bunkhouse to begin clean-up.

"Good luck," Libby whispered to Margalit as she ambled past.

"Thanks for everything," said Margalit. Brows furrowed in concentration, she was crouched at the side of her bed pinching and poking the sheet and blanket the way she had learned to do it by the light of a flashlight.

She smiled wryly to herself. In the limousine on the way up to camp, she'd worried about the kinds of girls there'd be in her bunk, about whether she'd be good at sports, even about whether she'd be homesick. Never in her remotest imagination had she dreamed that her biggest problem would be the attainment of perfect hospital corners on a bed!

Suddenly, the air was pierced by a shriek of agony. Miriam had bent over to reach the corner of her blanket near the wall, and she was having a hard time straightening up.

"Can someone give me a hand, please?" Miriam whimpered.

Tzippi promptly appeared at her side and jovially extended her hand. "One helping hand. At your service."

Miriam frowned. "Very funny, Tzipporah Laya, but I wasn't kidding," she protested unhappily, pressing her hand against the small of her back. "I think I have some kind of a cramp in my back."

Libby searched the cabin for Chedva, but she was nowhere in sight. Then she remembered what Margalit had told her in the morning.

Bustling over to where Margalit was industriously working

on the second corner of her bed, Libby tapped her friend gently on the shoulder.

"Think you could do that massage stuff you were telling me about on Miriam?" she asked. "She has some kind of a kink in her back, and Chedva doesn't seem to be around."

Reluctantly glancing over her shoulder at her unfinished housekeeping, Margalit followed Libby to Miriam's cot. She knelt at Miriam's side and started kneading the muscles of her neck, then her shoulders, and finally she worked her way down her back.

Miriam's taut muscles began to relax. "You're a magician!" she gasped in grateful relief. Clutching the bedpost, she very slowly pulled herself upright. "How did you know what to do?"

"Oh, that happens in the gym all the time," Margalit explained modestly. "Someone's always pulling something."

She flexed and unflexed her weary fingers. "It's either the fingers or the icebag," Margalit said, and she smiled shyly.

"That's right," Yehudis reminded herself. "You were supposed to show us some of your gym moves last night. We were so zonked, we forgot all about it! Want to do some now?"

Margalit was sorely tempted. But she had set herself a task, and she meant to complete it to the best of her ability.

"As soon as I finish my bed," she promised regretfully.

As Margalit trudged back to attend to her bedmaking, Libby mentioned casually to Nava, "Margalit's bed is starting to look much better, isn't it?"

Nava noted the electric blanket lying perfectly flat on the cot and grinned. "Now that the weather's warming up, maybe she sent her sheep pasture back to wherever it came from."

The innocent comment about the weather brought a

momentary scowl to Libby's generally sunny disposition. She willed the corners of her mouth to turn back up. "I've got Sweeping Detail today," she sighed. "See you later."

On the way to the cupboard to get the broom, Libby checked on Margalit's progress. She was thrilled to see that this time, Margalit's bed seemed to be picture perfect.

"Looking good, Margalit," Libby complimented as she passed by.

Margalit beamed at her with a shining face.

Okay, now that Margalit's problem is taken care of, it's time to attack my own, Libby declared to herself as she pulled the old wooden broom down from its hook and began to propel it vigorously around the floor. The dustballs flew as Libby assaulted them with a vengeance. All the while, she tried to puzzle out a way to clear up the misunderstanding that had arisen about her swimming ability.

"Just tell them! Just tell them!" the dust seemed to whisper as Libby swept it into a dustpan.

"How?" Libby stared into the dusty mess for the answer.

Of course, the dust wasn't really talking to her. Libby knew what the answer was. All she had to do was to climb on top of her bed after clean-up and shout to one and all, "I'm sorry I gave everyone the wrong impression, but I really *don't know how to swim!*" Then she'd be able to suit up with the rest of the gang and enjoy herself at the pool without a worry in the world. The direct approach was always best. She was determined to give it a try.

"Almost finished everyone? The bunk inspector's on the way up the hill." Chedva sounded the warning.

"Yup, we're all ship-shape," Tzippi crowed.

Shalva smacked her lips. "I can taste the pizza already!"

"We can't miss today!" Margalit gave her pillow a final fluffing.

Margalit stood proudly at the side of her bed. She was confident that the bunk inspector would not be able to find fault with her cot today.

Bunk inspection was well under way, and the inspector was still smiling. That was a very good sign. She strolled through the bunkhouse with her clipboard, checking the boxes on the chart. The beds had passed with flying colors. The bathroom passed. The cubbies passed. The closet passed. The elated girls were exchanging looks of victory as the inspector was reaching up to affix Bunk Achva's first 10 to the chart—when the mysterious ringing started.

It sounded like the buzzing of an ordinary telephone. The campers stared around the room in astonishment. There was no telephone in their bunkhouse. What could it be?

The bunk inspector was as intrigued as the residents of the cabin. She joined them as they tried to locate the source of the strange ringing.

"Could there be a fire alarm in here?"

"It doesn't really sound like a fire alarm. Those are so shrill and loud!"

"How about an alarm clock?"

"Why would an alarm clock be ringing like a telephone?"

Chedva glared suspiciously at Tzippi. "I hate to be *choshed biksherim*, but do you know what that is?"

"Wish I did, oh fearless leader, but the answer is, unfortunately, no!" Tzippi assumed a grieved expression. "*Choshed biksherim*, indeed!" she muttered loudly.

The sound seemed to be coming from the floor. The girls scrambled around on hands and knees trying to locate its origin. All of a sudden, Margalit gasped; she suddenly remembered a personal belonging of hers that was capable of making that sound.

It was something she hadn't seen since the first day of camp, and she had forgotten all about it. As she was racking her brains to figure out where, precisely, she had put that thing, the ringing stopped.

The bunk inspector was dawdling in front of the big chart affixed to the bunkhouse wall, her red pen dangling from her hand. Margalit was so eager to find out if, this time, the bunk had really achieved a perfect score, that she did something out of character for her shy self. She marched boldly up to the bunk inspector and asked her loudly, "So, did we get the 10?"

"Yeah, I guess you did," the bunk inspector answered, smiling.

As she pencilled a big red 10 onto the clean-up chart, Bunk Achva roared its approval. Libby stopped by to pat Margalit on the back.

"You finally did it!" she hooted.

But for some reason, Margalit was oblivious to the general merriment. She hovered close to the bunk inspector, trying to accelerate her movement through the cabin and out the front door. She had an unpleasant feeling that she knew where her noisy possession was. With a sense of dread, she had realized that it was keeping company with a whole crowd of other items that, if seen by the bunk inspector, might play havoc with the bunk's posted score.

Margalit knew she didn't have much time. The ringing

might start up again at any minute!

As the bunk inspector was just about to step through the door, Margalit's worst fears were realized.

"BBRRrrringgg . . . BBBRRrrrinnggg . . ."

"What *is* that?" The bunk inspector swivelled on her heels and rejoined the hunt.

Margalit crawled back to her bed as fast as she could. Diving underneath, she grabbed the receiver of her long forgotten cellular phone and whispered as quietly as she could, "Who is it?"

"Margie, is that you? We haven't heard from you in such a long time! Is everything okay?" the phone blared into Margalit's ear.

"Fine," Margalit breathed.

"Do you have laryngitis? What's the matter with your voice?"

Margalit knew that her parents were probably somewhere far away. She didn't dare have the *chutzpah* to tell them to call back at a more convenient time. What should she do? She despondently pulled a sweatshirt off her leg.

In the meantime, the stumped residents of Bunk Achva scratched their heads, perplexed. The ringing had stopped almost instantaneously this time. Was there a phantom telephone in the bunkhouse or was it just their imagination? And how could everyone be imagining the same thing, all at the same time? Chedva shrugged her shoulders and was escorting the bunk inspector out the door again, when a voice, low but unmistakable, could be heard coming from under Margalit's bed.

"No, really, there's nothing wrong with my voice. I'm having a wonderful time here. In fact, we're right in the middle of bunk inspection now. I have to go soon."

"Is that a new kind of game?" The bunk inspector could not contain her curiosity. This was the strangest cabin she had ever inspected. First, there was an invisible telephone ringing, and then someone was having a conversation with an imaginary person under her bed!

"Beats me," Chedva shrugged. "This hasn't happened before, so far as I can tell." She furrowed her brow to demonstrate that the morning's events seemed equally bizarre to her.

"Well, let's investigate then."

By now the rest of the inhabitants of the bunk were listening to Margalit's one-way conversation. They had no idea what to make of it.

"She's cracked up!" Shalva whispered to Tzippi, crossing her eyes.

For once, Tzippi was speechless. What *could* Margalit be doing talking to herself under her bed?

"No, we haven't gone swimming yet. It's been too cold. The counselor said we might be going this morning." Margalit was speaking in as muted a voice as she could manage, but her words carried clearly across the dead silence of the bunkhouse.

As the girls looked on in concern, Chedva and the bunk inspector tiptoed over to Margalit's bed and peered curiously underneath. Their eyes widened in shock as they caught sight of Margalit, cellular phone in hand, engaged in a *real* conversation. She was as comfortable as it was possible to be under a bed, reclining on a pile of wadded up clothing.

What Margalit had recalled in alarm, when she'd reminded

herself about the surprise her parents had packed in her suitcase, was that she had neglected to remove a whole bunch of overflow belongings from under her bed. The telephone was only one of them.

So, while she had been talking, Margalit had been desperately trying to shove the things under her bed behind her back. She had not been entirely successful. Discarded clothing was in evidence all around her, despite her well-intentioned efforts.

Margalit peeked out at the two counselors from her padded nest under the bed and smiled weakly. As they continued to stare at her, mouths hanging wide open, Margalit raised her hand and half-heartedly waved at them.

"What's going on under there?" Tzippi couldn't hold herself back. She bounded over in three immense leaps and stopped short, her mouth rounded into a perfect O.

The rest of the girls slowly trickled over to view whatever it was that was so astounding under Margalit's bed.

"I'm sorry, girls," the bunk inspector apologized when she had gotten over her surprise and straightened up. "I'm afraid I'm going to have to change the mark."

She hustled over to the chart, crossed out the beautiful red 10 and substituted a 9 instead. Then, shaking her head, she staggered out of the cabin.

Margalit continued talking to her parents for several more minutes. She had to reassure them that everything was really all right, when she knew for sure that everything in Bunk Achva was all wrong—again.

Mortally embarrassed, Margalit considered staying under the bed all day. Maybe she would even stay there all summer! It would certainly be better than having to face her disappointed bunkmates. She scowled at the skirts and sweaters she had kicked under the bed the first day and had forgotten about. Of all the times for the phone to ring, why had it chosen to ring at just the wrong moment?

"You okay?" Libby called into the silence under the bed.

The girls had waited patiently for Margalit to emerge from her mid-morning conversation so they could get the precise details of what was going on. Most of them had never seen a cellular telephone. When some time had gone by and Margalit had not appeared, Libby poked her head under the bed. Margalit was sobbing into a sweater.

"Aw c'mon, that wasn't your fault!" Libby consoled the distraught girl.

"So whose fault was it then?" Margalit sniffled dejectedly.

Tzippi bounced up and down in great excitement. "Hey, Margalit. That was really neat!" she chortled. "It was worth not getting a 10 to see the expression on that inspector's face when she caught sight of you under the bed, talking on the telephone! Even I, Tzippi the Magnificent, could never have pulled off such a great stunt!"

"You sure had us fooled!" Nava agreed passionately.

"How'd you get a telephone installed under your bed?" Chumi had never heard of a cellular phone. The only telephones she'd seen had been attached to the wall by sturdy cords. She slithered along the floor to try to get a glimpse of the unusual instrument.

Tzippi watched Chumi sliding along the floor and her eyes began to twinkle merrily. "Know how people get their telephones installed under their beds?" she asked in a melodramatic voice.

"Wait a minute!" Margalit interrupted, "You know cellular phones don't need . . ."

Tzippi flung her arm around Margalit, cutting off her explanation. "It's really quite interesting how they do these under-bed installations," she shouted.

"How do they?" Chumi was all ears. The other girls in the bunk drifted over gradually as Tzippi exuberantly launched into her strange tale.

"Well, it all started with the shaggy gray monster with the pointy fingernails," Tzippi declared solemnly.

"Huh?" All eyes turned to stare at Tzippi. What was she *talking* about?

"You guys, remember the night that Chedva got sprayed by the skunk?" Tzippi cackled.

Chedva groaned. "I'll never forget it," she grumbled.

"Yeah. Well, you know how we thought there was a creepy sinister gray creature lurking around underneath the bunkhouse that night, trying to poke his sharp fingernails through the floorboards?"

There was silence in the cabin as everyone tried to figure out what Tzippi was getting at. Even Margalit had stopped feeling sorry for herself and was listening intently.

Chedva puckered her mouth in annoyance. "And it turned out to be a skunk! Right?"

"Well, there was definitely a nasty old skunk under there," Tzippi agreed, "but the scratching was *so* loud, that maybe there was something else under there too!"

Miriam was doubtful. "Yeah? Like what?"

"Oh, any number of things," Tzippi teased.

"Name one," Miriam challenged.

Tzippi waited patiently until the suspense had mounted. "Does anybody believe that just *maybe* there was a despicable gray creature, with moldy hair and obnoxious bad breath, who was scuttling around under our bunkhouse that night?"

"Oh, please." Miriam rolled her eyes and made a face.

"Well?" Tzippi circled the floor and waggled her eyebrows at the rest of the group. "Some of you sure believed it that night! I know I did!"

The campers ruefully remembered their palpable fear. But now it was daytime. Shaggy monsters didn't have the same appeal in the light as they did in the pitch dark.

"So what was it already?" Chumi was getting tired of the game.

"Haven't any of you guessed?" Tzippi deadpanned. She paused dramatically, and then, when she was greeted by silence, she continued in a rush. "Why, it was Margalit's telephone installer, come to install her under-bed telephone!"

There were a few nervous titters, and then the bunkhouse suddenly exploded into hysterical laughter. The girls rolled around on the bunkhouse floor, holding their sides and trying to catch their breath.

"Why are we laughing?" Yaffa wondered as she was hit by another burst of hysteria. "That wasn't even very funny!"

"I think everyone's nerves were just on edge," Chedva diagnosed. She had mercifully not been afflicted by the mysterious laughing bug.

Margalit crawled out from under the pile of clothing beneath her bed. "No hard feelings?" she asked hopefully.

"Are you kidding?" Yehudis hiccuped. Her hand flew up to her mouth as she was overcome by a massive bout of hiccups.

Libby ran to the bathroom for a glass of water. She raced back and handed it to Yehudis as she gulped between hiccups. "Pizza . . . hiccup . . . we can get anytime. . . hiccup . . . Under-bed telephones . . . hiccup hiccup . . . are once . . . hiccup . . . in a lifetime . . . hiccup!"

"Okay, girls, calm down," Chedva announced. "It's time to get ready for swimming."

Chedva was always the voice of reason. She turned to Margalit. "Why don't you tidy up this mess once and for all," she suggested kindly, "and then join us at the pool?"

"I'll help!" Libby volunteered.

"You don't have to," Margalit assured her. "I can handle it myself."

"Oh, but I *want* to," Libby insisted.

Margalit shrugged. She inched her way under the bed and started dragging out rumpled skirts, sweaters, hair ribbons, belts, her balled-up sheepskin and a multitude of other assorted objects. Libby began folding and piling. The rest of the girls hurried to change into their bathing suits.

"Now what should I do with all this stuff?" Margalit ruefully recalled the last time she had posed that question.

"The same as you did with all the rest of it," Libby said. "Put the used things into your laundry bag. The stuff you need till Shabbos, stick into your cubby. We'll carry the other things over to the casino. We need to store the sheepskin there anyway—it's too big to keep in the cabin." Libby was a very practical person.

Carrying the odds and ends over to the casino served two very useful purposes, only one of which was to neaten up the bunkhouse. The other, more importantly, was to stall for time.

The casino was at least a five minute walk from the cabin, even longer when you were loaded down with bulky objects. At least seven or eight minutes to the casino . . . another five or ten to climb up into the attic and put everything into the suitcases . . . five minutes to get back. Libby smirked to herself as she mentally counted off the minutes.

By the time they were through, there'd be no time left to change into their bathing suits and get down to the pool before the activity would be over! Tsk, tsk! What a shame!

CHAPTER TEN

Ten Happy Campers

"Now *this* is an activity I can really get to like!" Shalva sat back on her heels as Tzippi dipped her oar easily into the water.

The two girls were paddling a canoe around the calm waters of Lake Tehila. The late afternoon sun streamed down on them from an almost cloudless sky.

"Yup! Next to sports, this is my favorite activity." Tzippi pulled her oar into the boat, and it drifted lazily on the current.

"This has been the best day so far," said Shalva happily.

She was in an unusually upbeat mood. There had been potato soup for lunch, with large chunks of real potatoes and fat bright orange carrots swimming in the oniony broth. Large baskets of garlic bread had been brought to the table to go with it, and even the talented cook at Camp Tehila had not been able to do much to ruin the pungent loaves. At rest hour, Shalva had slowly and lovingly enjoyed her last fruit.

Except for volleyball, during which Shalva had given her usual lackluster performance, the rest of the activities had been perfectly pleasant—swimming, arts and crafts and a mini-hike on the nature trail. And the weather was finally warming up. It was enough to make even a confirmed grouch smile!

"So, what's it like here on *Shabbos?*" Shalva trailed her hand in the dark green water.

"Oh, *Shabbos* you'll really like," Tzippi gushed. "It's very relaxing, if you know what I mean . . . we go to *davening*, there are a few *shiurim*, leisurely strolls along the road, *seven layer cake* . . ." Tzippi drew out the last three words so that Shalva could absorb the full impact.

Shalva licked her lips and looked pensive. "Think that was what was on the counter the night we tried to raid the kitchen?"

"Most probably. I couldn't see too well—the windows were kind of dirty—but it did definitely appear to be something of the chocolate frosted variety."

"Listen, Tzippi. We've got to figure out a way to get into the kitchen," Shalva exclaimed with great feeling.

"You're telling me!" Tzippi blustered. She gazed absently at the other canoes on the lake, which were starting to head back to shore. "I'm still working on it. But have faith. Old Tzippi never lets her friends down! Why, by next week, your stomach will be so full of chocolate cake, you'll hardly be able to move. *That* may be when you need the infirmary."

Shalva smiled in anticipation. "By the way," she noted, "it looks like the activity's over. All of the canoes are heading back to the boathouse. We're the farthest ones out."

"You kidding? Watch this!" Tzippi slipped her oar back into the water, motioned for Shalva to do the same and then called at the top of her lungs, "Last one back to the boathouse is a fibulated fishmonger!"

Shalva's eyes bulged as she watched what happened next. Tzippi's oar seemed to be moving at super speed. The little canoe spurted at breakneck velocity across the water.

"*Nu*? You sleeping? Move your paddle!" Tzippi ordered.

"Aye aye, Captain Zandberg!" Shalva saluted.

She was not a very experienced oarswoman, but she gave it her best shot. In utter disbelief, she watched their canoe passing one twosome after another.

"Obviously, *you* have no intention of being the fibulated fishmonger," Shalva observed with a chuckle.

"You don't either, if you're with me! Now get a load of this!" With a flourish, Tzippi turned the boat single-handedly and resumed her heavy duty rowing. She kept up a steady patter along the way.

"C'mon you guys! Get a move on! That's a canoe, not a paddleboat! You gonna let us beat you?" Tzippi continued her taunts while the canoe hurtled toward shore.

It was a tight race. Yaffa and Yehudis put up a valiant fight. They were leading all the way until about ten feet before the boathouse. Then, with one huge heave, Tzippi sent her canoe shooting straight for the dock.

As the four girls scuttled out of the canoes and dragged them to the boathouse, they scrutinized the lake and the canoes still on it, straining to see who would be the fibulated fishmongers.

Tzippi was twisting herself into a pretzel on the bunkhouse floor, trying to imitate some of Margalit's easier moves. "How'd you ever learn to do that?" she marvelled.

"It takes lots of practice," Margalit said, "and you have to limber up with all kinds of stretches." She was basking in the glow of the compliments she had received after her performance of the short gymnastics routine she had developed.

"You mean like . . ." Tzippi had a wicked glint in her eye. "*Bevakasha* . . . leg lifts?" She daintily pointed her toe and lifted her leg as high as she could, which was about waist height.

Margalit smiled. Instead of answering directly, she pointed her own toe and lifted her leg so high, it looked to the astounded campers as if it would break right off. Then she grabbed her ankle and hugged it against the side of her head.

"*Bevakasha*, leg lifts?" Tzippi gulped.

Margalit nodded her head. "We do about twenty minutes of warm-ups before every class," she explained patiently, "and then about the same amount to cool down at the end."

"I never thought I'd say this, especially after that torture we went through on the handball court yesterday." Yehudis wrinkled her nose in distaste at the memory. "But do you think you could teach us some of the important stretches?"

"We could do them at rest hour. It would be like our own private gym club," Miriam suggested.

"Ooh, that sounds so exciting!" Chumi bounced up and down on Margalit's bed. Margalit had generously provided her bed as seating for the audience.

"I am knowing good exercise, too," Olga announced, and to everyone's surprise, quiet Olga slipped down into a perfect front split, her legs forming a straight line on the wooden floor.

"Wow!"

"Look at all the talent in this bunk!"

"Didn't I tell you we had the greatest bunk in Camp Tehila?"

Tzippi boasted. "And that was even before we made all these extra discoveries!" She puffed out her chest in pride.

Margalit turned toward Olga. "What do you say about being my assistant coach?" she offered.

Olga beamed as Margalit gracefully extended her arms over her head, leaned into a back walkover and held it for a few seconds, so that her legs were split perfectly while she stood on her hands. Then she landed in a flawless front split beside Olga.

Olga flushed with pleasure. "Oh, I am liking this very much, thank you."

Margalit dimpled. Everything was just as she had imagined it would be, only twenty-four hours later than she had originally anticipated. In the meantime, so much else had happened!

She ruefully remembered squatting on the cold tiles of the bathroom in the middle of the night with the shower running to hide the sound of her sobs. Things had seemed so depressing then; she had even contemplated calling Albert the next morning to come and get her. She probably would have, if Libby hadn't intervened and helped her out.

Now, *baruch Hashem*, things were finally pulling together for her. There was not even a dustball left under her bed. Her cellular phone had been given a place of honor at the top of the bank of cubbies. And she knew how to make hospital corners as well as any of her bunkmates. Tomorrow, she was positive, the bunk would get an impeccable score at clean-up.

Climbing under her snug electric blanket after Lights Out, Margalit realized with a start that with the arrival of the warmer weather, it was no longer necessary for her to even switch it on. Soon she might go back to the casino and get her summer coverlet, she mused dreamily, as sleep began to overtake her.

Maria had packed her bags for all eventualities. When she had been consolidating her belongings on the second day of camp, Margalit had noticed that in the same duffle in which she had placed the dainty white eyelet summer cover, Maria had also included—an electric fan!

Libby was the last to fall asleep. Long after the final snippets of conversation had trailed off, and the cabin was filled with the peaceful sounds of steady breathing and the occasional snore, Libby was still tossing and turning in her bed.

"Why didn't I just stand up and tell them?" she agonized. "I had it all planned out while I was sweeping."

What she had done instead was to take the easy way out, again. Helping Margalit clean up under her bed had not been an act of total *chessed* on Libby's part. No, she had an ulterior motive in begging to be of service.

Margalit's unending gratefulness did little to soothe Libby's guilty conscience. When Margalit had apologized for the third time for causing Libby to miss swimming, Libby decided to tell her the truth. Just as she was working up the courage to spill her secret, the two girls had arrived at the casino with their load.

Sneaking up to the attic during the day did not prove to be as easy as it had been in the evening, when the place had been deserted. The casino was fairly jumping in the morning, with both sewing and art activities being held there simultaneously.

In the end, just Margalit crept in, since she had been there before and knew where to go. She had to make three trips, tucking just enough stuff under her T-shirt so as not to attract too much attention. The last ascent, balancing the bulky sheepskin, had been the most challenging.

By the time the two girls had completed their mission, more than half an hour had elapsed. Instead of enjoying a leisurely stroll to the bunkhouse, they had to hurry to the volleyball court. In all the rush, Libby forgot all about her intention of confiding in Margalit. When she finally remembered, Margalit had already been chosen for a team, and it was too late.

Now Libby was back to square one. Tomorrow would be a swimming day. She could feel it in her bones. And if she didn't manage to announce to one and all that, in fact, she couldn't swim, they would find out for themselves at the pool, and she would be mortified. How would she face them for the rest of the summer?

Libby briefly contemplated going into the bathroom, turning on the shower and hunkering down on the floor. After all, it had worked for Margalit! But what if nobody came? Or, even worse, what would she say if it was Chedva who showed up? Sighing, Libby thrashed about for almost another hour. By the time she finally did fall asleep, she was too tired to even dream.

Erev Shabbos dawned bright and sunny. The Bunk Achva girls had recuperated from the rigors of their Wednesday hike, and they greeted the day with renewed vigor. Spirits were high as the girls loped up the hill to their cabin after breakfast.

"So whaddaya say, partner, think we're finally gonna post a perfect score in this round of clean-up?" Tzippi warbled. She galloped at Margalit's side and jabbed her in the elbow.

Margalit grinned. "Well, I'll certainly give it the old one, two . . ." She punched the air for emphasis.

"Pizza party, here we come!" Shalva raised her fist in anticipated victory.

To stimulate the proper mood, Yehudis joined in with a victory song, as loud and as off-tune as her usual melodies.

As they entered the bunkhouse, Tzippi leaped onto a chair and solemnly announced, "Anyone with anything strange under her bed, kindly remove it immediately. That goes not only for telephones, but for pet salamanders (Yaffa had actually kept one under her bed last year), furry monsters, stashes of food or anything else that might get in the way of our *pizza party!*"

"Hear! Hear!" the girls called as they made their beds.

"If we can get seven perfect scores by next weekend, I figure next *Motzei Shabbos* we'll be having *some* party around here," Tzippi crowed, doing a little dance on her chair.

"If you don't get off that chair and get your own bed made right away, *you* won't be there," Miriam cautioned sweetly. "Go look at the chore chart and see who has bathroom detail today."

"Mumble, grumble. Foo and Pooh!" Tzippi muttered as she bolted off the chair. She hadn't checked the chore chart.

Margalit surveyed her bed from every angle. She leaned down and checked underneath. From her position on the floor, Margalit spied a tiny corner of her nightgown peeping from under the ruffle on her pillow. Swiftly, she vaulted up to poke it into place. When she had convinced herself that her bed and its surrounding area were absolutely immaculate, Margalit fetched the broom to complete her assigned chore.

As she propelled the broom past the bathroom door, Margalit covered her mouth with her hand to keep from bursting into uproarious laughter. Tzippi was entertaining herself as she performed her least favorite task.

"*Bevakasha!* Arm lifts!" Tzippi boomed as she swabbed at the toilet with a toilet bowl brush. "And one . . ." Bowl brush in hand, Tzippi raised her arm. "And two . . ." With a splash, she brought her arm rapidly down, so that the brush sloshed into the toilet. "And three . . ." As she was raising her arm again, Tzippi caught sight of Margalit in the doorway. She smirked. "Do they do warm-ups like these at your gym?"

The two girls exchanged amused glances. "You don't want to get out of practice," Tzippi invited cordially, holding the dripping toilet brush out to Margalit.

"No thanks," Margalit declined. "I have broom duty." She moved off to continue her sweeping, chuckling to herself. Who else but Tzippi could think of a fun way to swab toilets?

"Okay, girls, line up. The bunk inspector's on her way!" Chedva gave her customary warning and then, acknowledging the supreme effort the campers had made, added cheerfully, "And good luck!"

For the first time all week, bunk inspection went off without a hitch. There were no rugs to trip over, no clothes strewn about in unexpected places and all of the beds looked like they had been made by professional housekeepers. Even the bathroom passed, despite the mysterious puddles around the toilet. The cubbies passed. The closet passed. And, thank goodness, no telephones rang to distract the bunk inspector from affixing a brilliant purple 10 to Bunk Achva's clean-up chart.

The girls held their breaths until the inspector was out the door and safely down the steps. Then pandemonium broke out! Tzippi whooped. Shalva bounced up and down, the smell of warm pizza already filling her nostrils. Chumi and Nava hugged each other. Yaffa ran around the bunk pounding everyone on the back. Yehudis contributed a suitable party tune. Margalit sat on her bed, relief flooding over her in waves.

Libby decided that this would be a perfect time to make her announcement. So while everyone was in a jolly frame of mind, Libby perched on a chair and screamed into the chaos, "Hey, everyone, *I can't swim!*"

Nava elbowed Chumi. "Didya hear that? Libby can't *wait* to go swimming!"

"Well neither can I!" Chumi bubbled. "What are we waiting for? Swimming's first activity. Go grab your swim suit."

Chumi nudged Yaffa. "Libby missed swimming yesterday. She's in a hurry to get down to the pool."

Yaffa pulled her bathing suit out of her cubby and waved it in the air. "You guys! We'll celebrate later! Margalit and Libby didn't get to go swimming yesterday, and they don't want to miss even a minute of it today!"

"Don't worry, Libby. I'll be ready in a sec!" Tzippi promised, already halfway into her bathing suit.

"Me too!" Margalit rose from her flawlessly made bed and grabbed one of several bathing suits from her cubby.

Libby climbed down from the chair, confused and forlorn. She *had* told them she couldn't swim! She'd screamed it out at the top of her lungs! But nobody had been paying attention to her. As usual, her bunkmates had heard only what they expected her to say.

Having no choice, Libby slowly made her way to the bathroom with her swimsuit. She emerged just in time to join the rest of the gang on their way to the pool.

"So, Libby. Are you taking the deep water test today?" Miriam inquired. "If you want, I'll put your name on the list. I passed mine yesterday!" Proudly, she held up her wrist, which was circled by a bracelet of stretchy maroon material.

"What do you have to do to pass the deep water test?" Libby tried to control her nerves, but her voice was weak and shaky.

Miriam was so busy admiring her maroon badge of swimming ability that she didn't notice anything strange about Libby's tone. She looked up and explained, "First, you have to swim two widths of the pool, any stroke. I did one of breast stroke and one elementary back."

"Oh. That's swell!" Libby had no idea what either of those two strokes even looked like.

"Yeah. It was fun. And then you have to tread water for one minute."

"Anything else?" Libby was trying to commit the requirements to memory.

"Nope. That's it! It'll be a cinch for you!"

"Thanks. Listen, don't sign me up yet for today." Libby tried to think fast. "I can only swim in warm water. How was the water yesterday?"

Miriam gave a mock shiver. "Brrr. Actually, it was freezing!"

That's it! Libby sighed to herself in relief. Aloud she said, "Maybe I'll take a raincheck on the deep water test until the water warms up a little. I can't swim in ice cold water."

"Or warm water either, for that matter," she muttered.

"What'd you say?"

"I said, thanks for the offer." Libby felt like such a chicken. She couldn't confide in someone who'd just passed the test. Maybe she'd speak to Chumi over the weekend. Someone who could hardly swim might be more sympathetic.

The girls of Bunk Achva strolled to the pool as a group, but once they got there, it was every girl for herself. Gleefully, they joined the other campers already in the pool.

There was much splashing and general merriment. It was quite some time before anyone noticed that Libby didn't seem to be in the pool with them.

"Where's Libby?" Chumi was the first to notice. She had hoped to corner Libby in the water and elicit a few pointers.

Tzippi was about to execute a back dive from the diving board. She had also passed the deep water test yesterday. Chumi called to her, "Is Libby out there with you?"

Puzzled, Tzippi twisted around so that she was facing the pool. From her high perch, she had a good view of both the pool and the deck. Unfortunately, most of the swimmers were wearing bathing caps, and it was hard to tell one from another. Just as Tzippi was about to give up, she spotted Libby's golden hair fanning out on a beach towel on the deck. She indicated the general direction to Chumi, then sliced the water in a clean dive.

Chumi hoisted herself out of the water and padded over to Libby. Libby had smeared herself with suntan lotion and was happily baking in the sun.

"Aren't you coming in the water today?" Chumi bent down and poked Libby.

Libby reluctantly gazed up at her bunkmate, who was dripping cold water onto her leg. She stretched lazily.

"The water's just too cold today!" Libby said.

She was getting adept at using the excuse Miriam had put into her head. She tried not to think of what she could say next week, by which time the water would certainly have warmed up.

"Just sunbathing, then?"

"Yup."

"Want some company?"

"Sure!" Finally, here was Libby's opportunity to discuss her problem with Chumi. As she pondered how to get started, Chumi went to get her towel.

Before Chumi could get back, the lifeguards blew their whistles to clear the pool. Disappointed, Libby joined the stream of girls heading back to their bunkhouses to change for second activity.

"Hey, Margalit. I was just down at Mail Call to see if there were any letters for me. And there weren't!" Yaffa screwed her face into a hangdog expression.

"Oh, too bad. They'll probably be there next week," Margalit consoled sympathetically.

"Right!" Yaffa agreed glumly. Then she brightened. "But you should see what's down there for you!"

"Oh, goody!" Margalit jumped up, thrilled. "I haven't gotten anything since camp started!"

"Well, this is the biggest something you've ever seen!" Yaffa's eyes were as round as saucers.

"What is it?"

"You'd better come and see for yourself. I'll come down and give you a hand. You may not be able to manage alone."

"Ooh, I'm dying of curiosity. Give me a hint," Margalit begged as she laced on her running shoes.

"Well," Yaffa paused to consider, "it has two handles."

"Is it a pocketbook?" Margalit guessed. Then, remembering that Yaffa said it was very big, she corrected herself. "Is it a suitcase, maybe?"

Yaffa smiled mysteriously and pulled at Margalit's arm. "Close, but not exactly. Hurry up already!"

"Let's see. It's sort of like a suitcase," Margalit meditated as the two girls skipped down to the main house, "but not exactly. It has two handles, and it's very big." She was stumped.

Yaffa tossed out another hint. "It's beige, and it has a ribbon."

"Please, Sherlock, I can't stand the suspense!" Margalit implored. "Tell me what it is!"

"The truth is," Yaffa admitted, "I'm not sure what it is. I've never seen one before."

Margalit broke into a run, and Yaffa followed breathlessly behind. As they burst through the screen door of the main house, side by side, they both caught sight of the parcel at the same time. It was so big that it covered half of the desk in the office.

"Oh, you're finally here!" the office girl declared, relieved, when Margalit identified herself and claimed her package. "This came about an hour ago, and I didn't know where to put it."

"Wow! It *is* big, isn't it?" Margalit ogled the huge straw basket.

"You should have seen who brought it in!" The office girl gawked, impressed. "It was a guy wearing a uniform, like a policeman or something. And he said the funniest thing." She put on her best British accent, but it sounded more like an Englishman who had spent most of his life in Brooklyn. "He said, 'Please present this to Miss Margalit.' No last name or anything! I was so stunned, I forgot to ask him for the last name, and by the time I remembered, he was gone. Luckily for you, you're the only Margalit in camp."

Margalit smiled. Poor Albert! He had probably wanted to deliver the package to her himself. She suddenly felt homesick.

"Well, let's take it up to the bunkhouse already and see

what's in it!" Yaffa had almost forgotten that the package was Margalit's.

"Sure!" Margalit picked up one end of the wicker basket and Yaffa hoisted the other. The basket was not especially heavy, but it was bulky. The two girls struggled up the hill with it.

"Get a load of what's coming up the path toward our bunkhouse!" Tzippi exclaimed. She had been gazing out of the front window, trying to draw some inspiration for the letter she was writing. While inspiration had been slow in coming, the thing that was approaching now was moving at a pretty healthy clip.

Miriam heaved a sigh. "What is it now, Tzippi?" she asked in exasperation.

Tzippi was not to be deterred by Miriam's lack of enthusiasm. *She* hadn't seen the mammoth basket that was making its way up the path.

"Well," Tzippi exulted. "It's the biggest basket you've *ever* seen, and it needs *two* people to carry it!"

That was enough to draw most of the group to the window. Even Miriam put down her knitting and drifted over.

"Maybe it has a person in it!" Tzippi guessed.

"A person! Please! Have mercy!" Miriam rolled her eyes.

"Maybe there's food in there," Shalva whispered longingly.

"Maybe it's the hairy gray monster telephone installer!" Yehudis winked.

That provoked a round of chuckles. "Whatever it is, maybe we should give them a hand!" Nava suggested.

"Righto!"

"Definitely!"

"Let's go!"

En masse, they burst through the bunkhouse door and descended on the enormous basket, which had just begun to climb the steps. Yaffa had her back to the bunkhouse door, and they almost knocked her over in their enthusiasm.

"Hey, watch it, you folks!" Yaffa screamed as she struggled to regain her footing.

"Where are you all rushing to?" Margalit wanted to know.

The Achva bunch traded abashed glances. Finally Tzippi piped up, "We were just coming to help you!"

"Well, it sure took you a long time to get here," Yaffa grumbled. "My arms were almost pulled from their sockets."

"Oh, I'm terribly sorry. I didn't realize." Margalit was upset. "Why didn't you say something?"

"Only kidding," Yaffa grinned sunnily. "I wouldn't have missed it for the world. By the way, porters get first peeks inside." She nudged Margalit with her toe, since she was still holding the end of the basket with her hands.

"That seems fair!" Margalit beamed.

The entourage made its way into the bunkhouse, where Yaffa and Margalit set down the basket near Margalit's bed.

"Oh, I'm so tired." Margalit yawned noisily. "I think I'll open this after *Shabbos!*"

A pillow flew in her direction, and it was followed by a flurry of others.

"Mutiny!" Tzippi declared, retrieving her pillow and getting ready to toss it again.

"I do believe they want us to open it now," Yaffa observed with a straight face. "There's no rest for the porters of the world!"

Margalit was just as eager as the others to see what was

contained in her mysterious bundle. "I say we take a vote," she suggested coyly. "All those who say we open it after *Shabbos* say 'aye.'"

She was greeted by total and absolute silence.

"Well then, all those who vote that we open it *today* say 'aye.'"

There was a loud round of hoots and catcalls.

Margalit untied the checkered ribbons fastening the handles at the top of the basket. She peeked inside the basket and gasped at the treasure contained within. Yaffa was the second to get a glimpse. She opened her mouth in amazement.

"So, what is being in there already?" Olga could not restrain herself anymore. They gave her the third look. Her eyes widened and she licked her lips.

Finally, when the suspense was impossible to bear, Margalit lifted the cover of the basket and revealed a veritable feast. There was a huge chocolate layer cake in a plastic dome, an immense tub of melon balls, a bag of chocolate *rugalach*, a container of vegetable sticks with three containers of dips, a mammoth chunk of chocolate covered halvah and the biggest bag of all-dressed potato chips anyone had ever seen.

Attached to the basket's handle was a note that read, "For your first *Shabbos* in camp. Love, Totti and Mommy."

Scrawled in red below this message were the words "and Maria." In addition, a small note in blue ink read, "and Albert."

Margalit rubbed her eyes as tears streamed down her face. Why am I crying? she wondered. She could never remember being so happy.

"You know," Tzippi observed nonchalantly, "that does seem to be a lot of food for one person to eat all by herself."

"It is?" Margalit widened her eyes innocently. "I have a very big appetite!"

"We Torontonians," Shalva gulped, "would trade both of our moose and our whole lake of fish for a slice of that layer cake."

Libby caught on. "In Miami, we'd gladly swap a palm tree, four hundred coconuts and a beach full of seashells for a handful of all-dressed potato chips."

"I be giving you a big herring and a liter of borscht for halvah." Olga liked this game.

Margalit's smile lit up the whole bunkhouse. "Even though I have a very big appetite, there might be some leftovers for my friends."

Toes stubbed the bunkhouse floor uncomfortably as the residents of Bunk Achva recalled Margalit's unhappy start at camp. Which of them did she consider her friends?

Margalit watched the downcast eyes and shuffling feet. She knew that she had started off on the wrong foot, and it had gone downhill for a while from there. But that was all behind her now. *Shabbos* was coming, and then a whole new week would start. And she would be spending that time with the best bunch of girls she had *ever* met!

"And since *all* of you are my friends, we're going to have some *real serious eating* to do in this cabin over the weekend!"

This revelation was greeted by ebullient cheering. Pillows were airborne in celebration as ten happy campers hugged each other in glee.

Chedva had been quietly observing the entire exchange from her bed. Shaking her head in wonder, she joined the high-spirited group.

"You know," she told the girls earnestly when they had calmed down, "when I first came to camp, I figured they'd really goofed when they named this bunk Achva—brotherhood. I thought I'd never seen a more disunited bunch in my life. But I was wrong! In only a few days, you girls have made tremendous strides in learning how to get along with each other and help one another out. I can honestly say that Bunk Achva has pulled itself together and is finally reflecting its name! And I want you to know that I'm very proud to be your counselor!"

"Give her at least two slices of chocolate layer cake for that speech," Tzippi urged.

"And some melon balls!" Yehudis added.

"I volunteer one of my moose!" Shalva offered generously.

"Thank you. Thank you," Chedva applauded. "And now, everyone, please start lining up for your *Shabbos* showers."

As the Bunk Achva bunch readied themselves for *Shabbos*, chattering gaily, Shalva rolled her eyes and whispered to Tzippi, "If that's what Margalit's parents send her for her *first Shabbos*, imagine what they'll be sending for her second!"

But Libby couldn't bring herself to think about chocolate cake. She had other things on her mind. The deepwater test was fast approaching, and Libby's dreadful secret was *bound* to be discovered.

Read all about Libby's Deepwater Dilemma in Regards from Camp, Episode #2!